SY 0016263 9

D0551580

823.9
MUL
39635

A Friend of Don Juan

By the same author:

A TIME OUTWORN

A PEACOCK CRY

ANTIQUITIES

AN IDLE WOMAN

THE SUMMERHOUSE

VERY LIKE A WHALE

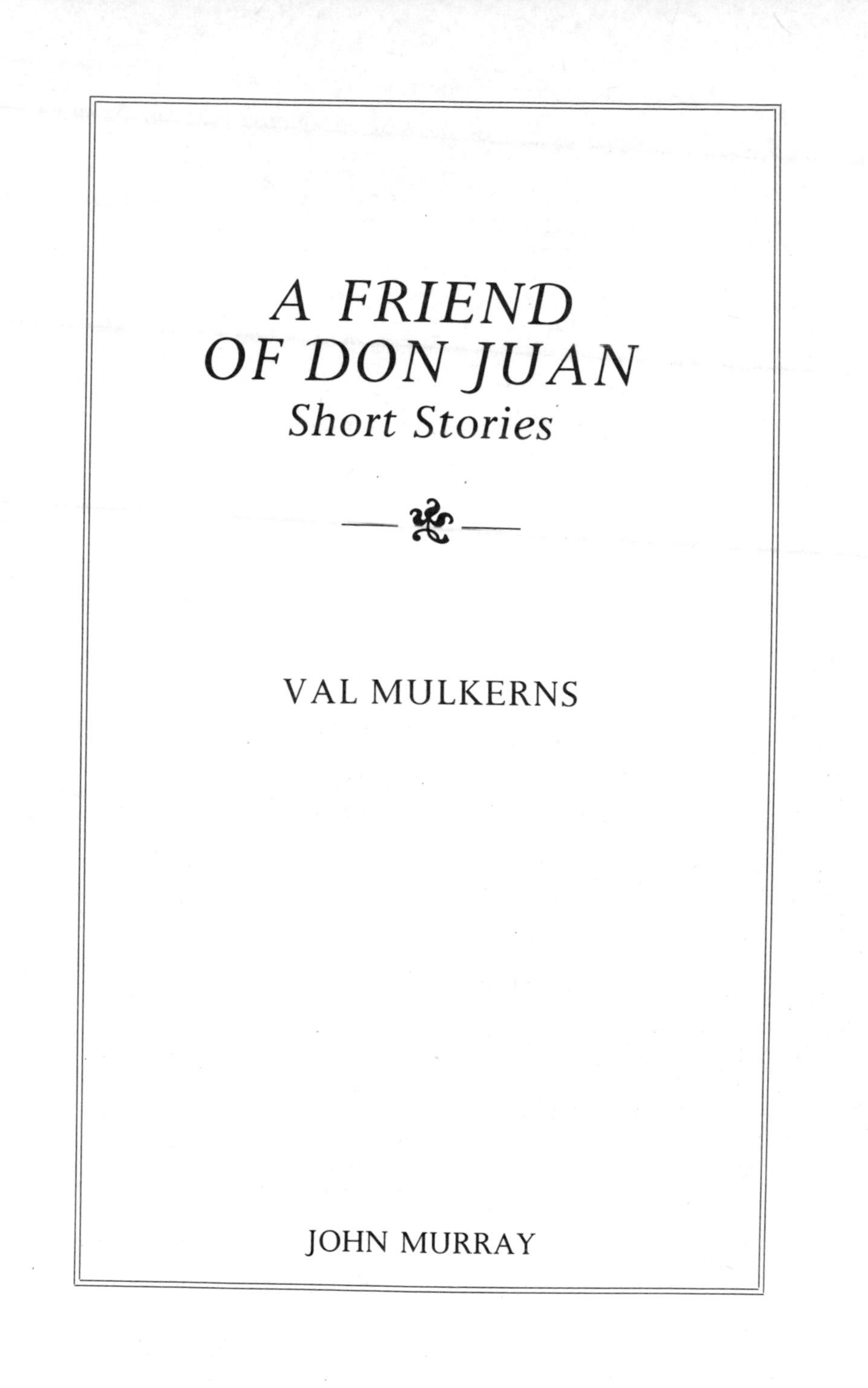

A FRIEND OF DON JUAN

Short Stories

VAL MULKERNS

JOHN MURRAY

First published 1988
by John Murray (Publishers) Ltd
50 Albemarle St, London W1X 4BD

Typeset by Inforum Ltd, Portsmouth

Printed and bound in Great Britain by
Butler & Tanner Ltd, Frome and London

British Library Cataloguing in Publication Data

Mulkerns, Val
A friend of Don Juan.
I. Title
823'.914[F]

ISBN 01–7195–4617–6

for KENNE-HOM
with admiration

Contents

Acknowledgements

Acknowledgements are made to The Poolbeg Press (who originally published 'Humanae Vitae', 'Still Life', 'The Open House' and 'Memory and Desire'), and to the Arts Council of Ireland, also to Macmillan and Co., Rias Radio Berlin, Radio Stuttgart, and Radio Telefís Eireann, and *The Irish Times* and *The Irish Press*.

the calm between storms
is the silence in which
the dead are not named
until relatives are informed

Dennis O'Driscoll, 'Brief Lives III' from *Hidden Extras*

The Honda Ward

IT WAS the middle-aged nurse this time, the one with the double chin and she shook her head regretfully. "No love," she said, "you're not due another for half an hour. You'll never feel it passing. Sister will be along to you then."

She went from him with her awkward long-assed walk to the newest arrival from the recovery room and he lay cursing and writhing in his pain, possessed by it as though it were a second skin. It began in his pelvis and throbbed down into his legs (what was left of them) and then in a moment the worst phase began, the feeling of steel jaws closing over his entire body. He ground his teeth and moaned, throwing his head from side to side of the pillow and he could feel the blood trickling from his lower lip where the teeth had bitten into it. He didn't know how long it lasted; it might have been hours. When the steel jaws began to close over him again he threw pride to the four winds and howled and at this point, as though straight on cue, his sister came in carrying daffodils. She took one look at him, dropped the flowers and tapped angrily across in her high heels to the nurse in the corner.

"I insist on seeing Sister this minute!" he heard her angry voice and the nurse said calmly: "Insist away. She'll tell you no different. He's not due another injection for half an hour."

Fidelma came running over to him and kissed his burning forehead. "I'll not let that cold bitch get the better of me. Be back to you in a minute, love!"

He gave himself up to the pain then, rolling and writhing with it, letting it split him in two and watching in his mind the two bleeding parts lying together side by side in the bed. He wished the surgeon had never put his legs together again. He wished he had never been picked up from the base of the lamp-post and carried gently to the ambulance. Lying there, before anyone came except that woman who had covered him with her fur coat and then gone shivering to the phone, lying there after it happened he had no pain. It was as though his entire body had been given one of those dental injections which freeze your gum. He felt nothing, totally out of touch with his body. He hadn't tried to get up because he didn't know where his legs were. How long ago? A week? Ten days? Longer? There was all that time in Intensive Care. He must ask Fidelma when she came back. He had forgotten to ask his father last night. It might even have been something to talk about. His father tended to go on looking at him in pity, finding very little to say.

He was between the steel jaws again, thrashing his head from side to side when Fidelma came back with the black-eyed Ward Sister who always seemed to be on the point of smiling. She brushed back his hair with a cool hand and looked sharply at him, "I'll have you right as rain in two minutes, Bonzo," she said, and walked elegantly away. It was five minutes, Fidelma muttered angrily, before she came back and even then she did not carry a hypodermic syringe but two white tablets on a little dish. "Get these down you now, James and they'll see you through to the next injection," and then he let himself go and hissed SHIT at her, although she only smiled back with great sweetness at him. He downed the useless things then, closed his eyes and tried to master the pain for Fidelma's sake. He imagined himself floating down a river with fire on either side of him, burning oil slicks maybe, although what would they be doing on a river? If he held his body tightly together the flames might not reach him. After what seemed a long time he floated free of the flames and there were tall yellow irises instead and cool river weeds on every side of him. He opened his eyes and saw Fidelma was crying a bit.

"I'm O.K. Fiddle, swear it. Never knew the little white buggers to work before."

"Great!" she said, smiling at him, her eyes dry in a moment. She started to arrange the daffodils in a vase on the window sill and she threw some dead ones in a bucket before sitting down again.

"All the gang were asking for you, Jim," she said. "They'll be in to see you tonight – well some of them."

"What day is it?"

"Friday."

"Oh God, Friday! Then it's two weeks since –"

"Yes!"

"I still have two legs, did you know that?"

"Did I know? Jesus, didn't we stay up all night. Dad and I! The first word that came over the phone was that you'd probably lose the left one, and Dad was wracked with tears the same as me before they phoned again. Mr Ryan had been called in out of his bed and saved the left one. Then we didn't care anymore. Dad made whiskey punch for the pair of us and we went to bed."

"Punch? Dad?"

"There you are now, he did. He'll be in to see you this afternoon as well. Early he says, and the lads will come later. I have to go now or I'll miss my French class."

When his father came he was shyly pleased to see the improvement and Jim didn't tell him that the injection was only ten minutes old. Some neighbours had given his old man a holy medal for poor Jim to wear around his neck and he didn't reject it out of hand. Reaching out, he put it beside the fruit on his locker and he could see the effort it took his father to refrain from repeating that the medal was to be worn around the neck on the cord provided.

"How's the form anyway?" his father repeated. He had a habit of repeating everything.

"Great, Dad," he said. "Tell me about the bike."

"She's not as bad as you might think. I've got her home now, of course, and now that you're a bit better I'll have the heart to check her carefully over the weekend. The front fork is distorted, of course, and the tyre is in ribbons and the rim is so far out of true that it will probably mean a new wheel, but we'll get over that. By the time you come home, Jim, I'll probably have her in good order again."

Even as the father spoke, he felt he was being treacherous to his daughter who had strongly argued forgetting about the bike, selling it for scrap rather, and lodging the proceeds to James's savings account. He felt it was too early yet to make such a sweeping decision on his son's behalf.

His limited store of small talk was almost exhausted when the first of the Honda crowd came spilling into the ward. Each of them pulled off his helmet and laid it down carefully along by the wall before turning to greet Jim. The father took his leave.

"How's it going? How's the fella then?"

There were five of them in big bikers' boots and they were bursting with health and red-cheeked from the cold outside. They all seemed taller than he remembered and they made him feel nervous, even defenceless. If in one of their scufflings they fell on his bed and knocked over the cage which protected his legs who knows what might happen? He looked up at the white mountain the cage made in front of him and he knew it was kept in place by tightly tucked bedclothes and that he was being neurotic to feel threatened. Yet he listened to the shop-talk of school and sport and wild weekends as though he were an outsider and older and all this had nothing to do with him and never would have again. Two of them squatted on the floor, the rest had borrowed chairs and sat happily around him. Nobody, he was thankful to note, tried to sit on his bed.

"Sparky is brillo these last few practices," Harding was saying. "Macker is trying him out for wing three-quarter. He might make the final in Lansdowne if he keeps it up."

"Not a chance!" Fanning said. "Too lazy, too fond of the booze and the birdies. It'll be Kennedy again like last year."

"The knee is not right yet," Fahey reminded them. "Kennedy has to keep it quiet for a while yet."

"He's started training again," Brown said. "Saw him jogging past the house this morning."

As they talked, they casually devoured his apples, his grapes and his chocolates and they were just about to pass around his fags when he had to stop them.

"You'll be thrown out of here if you light up fellas," he said. "Take them away if you want to – I've no taste for them since it happened."

Fanning winked and pocketed the fags and then they began to talk about school. Feeler, the History master, was going to be posted to another Jesuit house – in Siberia most likely, Brown leered and they all guffawed knowingly.

Stop it, he said, stop it for fuck's sake. But no words came out of his dry lips. The closing steel teeth of pain had started up again. Go away, he said to his mates. Go AWAY. But they went on. Gossip, news, gags he had to hear about. Fighting the pain, he found himself thinking about his mother for the first time in a while, wishing she could come through that door. She had been tall, even gangly and leggy like an overgrown schoolgirl and she had hardly ever stopped talking. Except when you were sick, that is. Then she had always known what to do, how to calm you, exactly what food to bring up and even what to say to raise a laugh and make you forget your miseries. She had thickly fringed grey eyes whose expression he could no longer recall and very white teeth but also a nose that looked like a boxer's and would never cause anybody to describe her as pretty. Yet she was dark and glossy and her perfume used to hang around after she was gone. She was gone a long time now – two years? He thought he was fifteen when she died and Fidelma thirteen. Fidelma was a bit like her to look at, except she had a nicer nose and Fidelma too could sometimes know exactly what you were thinking and do the right thing. Like today. He remembered fellows in school giving out about their old dears and not knowing what they were talking about. He wished she could have walked in through the door today instead of Fidelma. Would she have said something to make him laugh instead of cry? The steel jaws gripped him again and he beat his head from side to side and Fanning's big voice grated into his ear:

"Are you O.K. Lowry? Look we better be going, old son. Get you the nursing bird on the way out, O.K.?"

"See ya, Lowr," he heard one after another of their voices saying and then he heard the trampling of their boots and the rattle of their helmets as they took them up from the corner inside the door and clattered away down the corridor.

Sometimes he didn't even try to stop the tears dripping down his face and this was one of those times. He looked at his watch and knew he would have to wait fifteen minutes for another injection. Afraid of making him a junkie, they were. They were carefully rationing out the only thing that was any good to him, morphine. This time it might be administered by Beckett again. Nurse Beckett was from the North and she had told him her name was Caroline. She was a student nurse, really, not yet qualified and she wasn't much older than he was himself. He would surprise her by not moaning like a dog and thrashing about but facing the pain head on and besting it. His tears had dried on his face and there was five minutes to go.

"My aren't we the brave wee lad today and no mistake!" Caroline said, coming on him unawares. "How are we then?"

"Lousy, thank you," he grinned up at her.

"I'll have to give you another bed bath so," she said archly, and he found himself blushing which annoyed him so much that he forgot the pain. He had found it odd, in the beginning, during his rare moments of lucidity to find himself being intimately yet impersonally touched by women young and old in the ordinary course of their day's work. They might have been polishing furniture for all it mattered to them he often thought. It didn't matter even when he had to urinate into a tube for them and let them unstrap the bag from the bed and carry it away to be emptied. It didn't matter now that he had graduated to a bottle which had to be requested each time. But today when Caroline exposed his left buttock for the injection he coloured slightly and wondered if it was accidental that her little finger brushed his limp penis as she was settling back the bedclothes.

"Stay awhile and talk to me," he said to her.

"Is it hanged, drawn and quartered you'd have me James?" she murmured. "There's a wee crabbed bitch out there waiting to jump on me, so there is and I'll not give her reason. Mebbe tomorrow, though." She winked at him and went bouncing off on her flat heels, pink-cheeked and grinning, a few curls of brown hair ringing her cap at the back as he looked after her. Nineteen, twenty? Seventeen like himself? Tomorrow he'd ask her.

After his meal the last person he ever expected to see coming through the door to visit him was Feeler, but it couldn't possibly have been anybody else, he thought, even allowing for the spaced state he was in. Nobody but Feeler had that sharp-nosed country look under the thatch of sandy hair, the crooked teeth white as a hound's, the small limp womanish hands that seemed as though they ought to belong to somebody else. Feeler settled himself comfortably in the only armchair after a damp handshake.

"How's the boy?" he asked. He had a midland accent, soft and flat, and the big froggy pale-blue eyes rested sympathetically on the patient.

"Fine, sir."

"Have you any pain still?"

"Usually, yes. But they've fixed me up for the time being with an injection."

"The wonders of science," Feeler smiled. "The wind outside would skin a weasel, so you may as well enjoy the bed while you can." So far so clichéd, the boy thought. But something about the confident way this man filled the chair and looked across at him under the sandy fuzz suggested that he would not go away without saying something that you could remember.

"You won't thank me for it, but I've brought you a bit of work, Jim." He reached down into his briefcase, took out a few pages and laid them on the tray in front of James. "Work away on these whenever you can and send the finished job into me by one of the visiting fellows. You'll be well back on your feet before the exams and you won't want to be left behind by the rest of them. After all, it wasn't your brain suffered in the smash, was it?"

"Sometimes I'm not so sure," the boy muttered, a vague feeling of animosity suddenly coming like a cold wind between them. He didn't want to work in bed. Nobody else had suggested he should. And Feeler after all was on his way out.

"They tell me you'll be leaving us soon Sir?"

"True enough," Feeler said indifferently, "but one way or another that needn't bother you. I'm here until the end of the summer term and I see no reason why we shouldn't try to get you through your bloody exams."

"Thanks, Sir, I'll do what I can with the questions, but my writing is a bit worse than usual since it happened. I hope it won't drive you mad."

"Don't bother your head about that. My own handwriting gets more and more like the path home of a drunken spider. I'll manage yours fine. Anything bothering you?"

Again the look was sharp under the sandy hair, the almost white eyebrows. The boy didn't really understand why he wanted suddenly to talk to this odd man.

"Could you – could you tell them to keep the Chaplain out of my way, Sir? I haven't the guts to do it myself and they might listen to you. I couldn't really discuss it with my father. He left in this to me," and the patient indicated the medal on the table beside him.

"Maybe I'll find a good home for that," Feeler said, scooping it into his pocket and then fixing on the boy his bland-eyed country-cute look he asked:

"What's the holy man done to you, James, to incur your displeasure?"

"Oh nothing much, really – it's just that –" he looked down frowning at the blue bedspread, selecting his words carefully. "It's just that he was there looming over me (he's a big heavy man) when I was carted in, not knowing properly where I was and he kept nagging at me to make a good confession. He'd been sitting there when the two surgeons were talking about me, after I'd been given the injection. For a long time it took no effect because the Chaplain leaned over and said that the doctors as a general rule did a good job on fellows like me but of course nothing was certain and it was his duty as God's minister to be here ready and willing to give me absolution of my sins if only I'd make a good confession before being carried in to the operating theatre. Some people dying on the side of the road never got the chance and I was one of the lucky ones. A good act of contrition now after I'd confessed my sins would put me right with God if it so happened He wanted to call me this very day, did I understand?"

"Jesus wept!" exploded Feeler. "He said that to you and you flat on your back waiting to go in to the theatre?"

"Yes he did, Sir."

"And he frightened you into confessing?"

"No." Jim was smiling now. "But he did, I suppose, frighten me. They had to come back and give me another injection and they seemed surprised that I hadn't gone drowsy. After that I don't remember too much except the anaesthetist telling me to count backwards from ten and before I'd finished I was back in bed somewhere else, in Intensive Care as it turned out, and it was over."

"Have you seen the man since?"

"No, but Lent will soon be starting I hear, and it struck me he might try again. I'd rather not see him anymore."

"No bloody wonder. I can promise you you won't. Of course it might be regarded as none of my business but you've no mother and I'm going to speak to the old Matron on my way out. The man should be packed away sharpish out of here before he can do any more harm. Leave it to me, Jim."

"Thanks, Sir. I could make a bit of headway with the questions if I had my textbooks in the locker here. I'll ask Fidelma to bring them in."

"No need, fella." Feeler leaned in to the briefcase again

and then put the textbooks on the bedside table. "Fire away with these, maybe early in the mornings next week, if you can sit up a bit by then. See how you get on. I'll be in to see you again anyway. If you're not able for the whole effort, don't worry – I'll be talking to you about it again. Keep the old heart up now!"

Feeler made a last swoop into the briefcase and hauled out two packets of potato crisps, ten fags and a couple of Mars bars before he fastened it up and was gone, leaving the patient smiling in the direction of the door.

Half an hour later, in the valley time between tea and the bulk of evening visitors, he stared in disbelief at the large familiar priest bearing down on him from that same door. This time the man was dressed in a black polo-neck sweater and anorak and he was rubbing his huge hands to indicate the cold of outdoors.

"Lucky man to be where you are tonight, James. 'Twould freeze the marrow of your bones out there. How are you?"

Recoiling with every functioning muscle in his body, the boy stared at the closely shaved pink face, the grizzled hair cut close and bristling, the round black-rimmed glasses whose dazzle from the bedside lamp fortunately hid the eyes. Trapped, all he could think of doing was to close his eyes and lie there as though dead. The pain which had been dormant started to pulse through him again.

"Come on Jimmy, you were bright enough when I came in. God is good, and believe me there's a world of difference between the bright lad I saw and I coming through that door and the poor fellow carted in off the road in bits two weeks ago. God has been very good to you Jimmy, and don't you forget it."

Still he kept his eyes firmly shut, willing himself elsewhere, willing the loathsome hearty voice to go away. He willed it so hard that he half-thought God had indeed been very good and struck the man dumb to grant the sinner James this blessed silence. Furthermore he had not been touched, but then, it would have been quite difficult to touch him. He had snatched his hands instinctively under the bed-clothes on the priest's arrival and he lay there tense and motionless until he felt the heavy hand on his forehead. The words of the blessing had hardly ended when he opened his eyes and said deliberately "Fuck off, Father."

The priest pretended not to hear and sat heavily down by the bedside. Trembling after his effort, the boy closed his eyes again, pain strumming now in every part of his body. He tried to remember So all day long the noise of battle rolled among the mountains by the winter sea and when it failed there was Ride a cock horse to Banbury Cross and How many miles to Babylon and anything to keep the loathsome noise away, but it kept thickly breaking through. God was merciful but he did expect a little in return. Remember the healing of the ten lepers. His sense of Divine Justice was outraged when only one came back to give thanks. His patience was not infinite and if people who had been granted great favours didn't turn to Him (worse, if they turned away from Him) then God would not be mocked. Again, as on the day when James had been carried in on a stretcher to this hospital, absolution was now offered to him (God was merciful too remember, ever ready to forgive if only His creature would confess his sins and be sorry for them). He James, to whom God had been so good, had not only refused initially to make his peace with Him, but had actually schemed to try to ensure that the sacramental grace of a good confession would not be offered to him again.

In a sudden burst of decision the boy leaned painfully up and rang the bell behind his head several times, still without looking at the priest. The big man got to his feet and made a gesture of blessing just as a young student nurse came through from the main ward, exchanged a joke with her and went rambling away to the rest of the patients in the Honda ward.

"I think I'm going to be sick," he said to Nurse Beckett.

She fetched him the small plastic kidney-shaped dish and held him while he filled it. She wiped his mouth as he lay back quivering. She smiled at him, then poured him a glass of the glucose drink, which she gave him with two white pills.

"Here Jim," she said. "Put back a little of the liquid you lost that time. You'll feel the better of it, so you will."

He did too. He felt ready to hold her to her promise of talking to him even if it was not tomorrow yet. The pain gradually receded again.

"Do you never get browned off with all the horrible whining sick people you have to deal with?" he asked her and she shook her head with great energy.

"Never. Some of the well ones are a deal worse, I can tell you, naming no names." She winked and then he knew she meant the chaplain and a great grin spread all over his face. "There's them around the place I'd give the bum's rush to if I'd any say in it so I would, but I haven't. Three years to go or maybe four if I do my midwifery and then I'm away to Canada like the devil was at my heels, same as my sister. Alberta Canada here I come, fast as I can make it!" She giggled and hooked the straps of imaginary dungarees with her thumbs.

"What will you do there, Caroline?" She'd never actually told him that he could use her name but she obviously didn't mind.

"Work in one of the rich private clinics probably. That's where you make the bread AND meet mining millionaires. Mebbe even private nursing in big houses if I take the notion."

"I don't think there's too much private nursing in people's homes anywhere in the world now," he said. "But why not the States?"

"My sister says Canada is nicer and it's easier to get to know people. Sure I'm mebbe kidding about the millionaires. But I like people to be friendly and I love plenty of money in my pocket, not that I know too much about it. What will you do?"

"Haven't a clue. Can't see much beyond my Leaving if I ever get it after this. You need about forty points to have any choice of faculties in college."

"You could mebbe do a bit of work in bed instead of gosthering, couldn't you?"

"I mean to," he said.

"Tell you what," she said suddenly, "I'll take you for a wee walk – see some of the other star acts before the visitors come. Be back in a wink."

She returned with a wheelchair, and the pain as she helped him into it nearly made him faint but he held on.

"When the stitches are out, Jim, it will be better. The physiotherapist will make your joints work properly again and you'll be right as rain. Easy now."

She whirled him through onto the main part of the Honda ward of which he had seen only one small corner through his door. He was supposed to be a semi-private patient but nobody had come to replace the fellow who had gone home from his room. Out here there were twelve patients round about his own age, some of them sitting up reading copies of *Bike*, several with legs strung up and suspended from a pulley at the end of the bed, some with bandaged heads or arms, some lying flat with spinal injuries and all cheerfully, it seemed, resigned to their lot. The fellow they paused beside offered him a cigarette and Nurse Beckett turned her back obligingly, saying she would come and fetch him later on. The fellow's name was Dave and he had a broken pelvis and two broken wrists. His fingers emerging from the plaster were bluish but he could hold the biking magazine all right. "Look at this three-cylinder job – isn't she a beaut? They say she's got a vicious power band but that the frame and brakes are the best yet."

"She's all that. A rich guy in school was given one the same last year by his old man. Hasn't come off her yet!" Dave grinned with his white chipped teeth. "Give him time, mate. What was your problem anyhow?"

"Gave a guy a lift home from school and he didn't know how to go WITH her around a corner. Huge heavy boots.

Things went completely out of control and I hit a lamp-post."

"What about the passenger?"

"Not a scratch on him, and he hadn't even got a helmet."

"The way the cookie crumbles," Dave said indifferently.

"What about yourself?"

"Got a better run for my money than that," he grinned amiably. "Asking for it you might say. Seven or eight pints in me one Saturday night and I was coming home at a fair old wallop on the Bray road. That's all I can remember. The buzz of going well. Seems I encountered a Merc somewhere around the Kilcroney crossroads. Damaged her pretty paint quite a bit, I'm glad to say, but of course the driver wasn't scratched. They seldom are."

Jim nodded silently, impressed by the seven or eight pints bit. "Will you take her out again?"

"You kidding? Can't wait to get out of here and back on to her again. Haven't been without wheels since I was fourteen and you can bet your shirt I won't be going back to a push-bike at seventeen. Not a chance!" He was, he said, an apprentice electrician and he was saving up for a big job when he was out of his time. "You quitting?" he said to Jim then, who shrugged.

"Hard to say. There'll be a bit of pressure from home. Don't know how I'll feel about it when the pain stops and I can walk again."

"You'll feel fine about it."

"Expect so." Jim wished Beckett would come back and take him away as the first of the helmeteers arrived in a blast of sound. The steel teeth had started to close again around his thighs and he knew his face had gone white as he dug his nails into the palms of his hands. Dave was quick to notice his condition despite the fact that two of the visitors were for him.

"Hey," he said to one of them, "put this guy back in Millionaires' Row and make a bit of room for yourselves. See ya, Jim."

"See ya." The fellow who had wheeled him in looked down concerned at him.

"You O.K.?"

"Sure. Give that bell a buzz before you go, could you?"

"Will do." The big freckled redhead ambled off in his biking boots, and Jim could hear the guffaws of laughter coming in from there and see the drifts of smoke curling upwards. It seemed like half an hour before Beckett came running in to him, fixing a pin in her cap and full of apologies.

"Hold on there Jim till I get Nurse Keogh to give me a hand. Then we won't hurt you."

The two nurses seemed to flip him deftly out of the wheelchair and on to his bed where he lay back quivering.

"Mebbe we rushed you a bit, Jim," Beckett said. "Next week you'll be better able for this, won't he Nurse?"

"Sure," Nurse Keogh said, patting his shoulder before she hurried off.

"A cup of coffee just for this once," Beckett said.

"Love one, Caroline," he managed to smile at her and that was what helped him over the next hour of visitors. Last of all his father came, bearing a pink primula in a pot from the neighbour who had sent him the holy medal.

"Mrs Fahey says she's having a mass said for you on Thursday," his father told him. "Isn't that very good of her? And she says she'll ask Fr O'Dowd who's the Chaplain here to keep a special eye on you. He's a second cousin of her husband's. She says to tell you that she's sorry the arthritis keeps her from visiting you herself."

"Dad will you do something for me? Thank Mrs Fahey for her kindness and for the plant but tell her to keep the second cousin of her husband's as far away from me as possible – if she can."

"How could I bring a nice neighbour an extraordinary message like that? What would your poor mother say if she could only hear you?"

"She'd understand – Christ I could TALK to her," Jim burst out, already regretting it. "Sorry Dad, forgive me, but I do NOT want to see the hospital Chaplain anywhere near this bed ever again. If he comes I won't speak to him, any more than I did today. That's all."

His father looked baffled and anxious and quite obviously hadn't an idea how to handle it.

"You see Dad, I'm just not on the same wavelength as Father O'Dowd and the thing is you feel TRAPPED in bed by somebody like that who can just walk in and out as he pleases, invading you. I'm sorry if this worries you but you can forget what I asked you anyway. I'll deal with it myself. Or with a little help from my friends," he grinned in further apology.

"I simply don't understand you, James," his father said. "Maybe it's all those drugs have you upset."

"Maybe that's it. Thanks for coming in, Dad, and thank Mrs Fahey for the lovely plant and tell her not to trouble herself about the Chaplain – because we see him all the time. O.K.?"

"That sounds fair enough," his father said, though it was obvious that he was far from satisfied. "How's the form today otherwise?"

"Great. I was up for the first time today in a wheelchair – how about that?"

"Splendid, son. Fidelma has a maths grind tonight and can't come, but she'll be delighted when I tell her."

"And I had a visit from Father Duncan our history teacher. He brought in some work and he's going to make sure I don't become a layabout in here."

"I see," said his father, doubtful again. "Did you know Father Duncan is leaving at the end of next term?"

"Oh yes – more's the pity. He's a great teacher."

"I'm sure he is," said his father. "One has doubts about his suitability all the same."

"All gossip," Jim said firmly and he looked kindly at his father for the first time. He felt a great deal older than the grey-haired man looked and he felt that eventually he would be able to spare him an amount of worry about things the man would never be able to understand.

Humanae Vitae

AFTER rain, the washed blue sky glittered above the choppy sea, but the east wind was cold. "See," the man in the sheepskin coat said smugly, "I brought that bit of sun with me." Clichés were so seldom used as opening gambits that the wife glanced sharply at him before smiling.

"I could show you the Mass rock I wrote to you about," she said with some diffidence, at last. "It's better in the very late evening, just before sunset, but it may be raining by then."

"Almost certainly. So show me. Not more than seven miles there and back."

"It's much less, honestly. Michael and I did it a few nights ago before his bedtime. Mrs O'Friel puts the others to bed for me whenever I want to go out."

"Nice Mrs O'Friel. I liked her immediately."

Once again the wife glanced up, surprised and pleased, as she tried to measure her quick strides to his slow ones over the rocky fields behind the house. "She was delighted when she heard you were coming up for the last week – you wouldn't believe the fuss there was the last few days. She wanted to know would I like to change my room when the Flynns went because the wardrobe was bigger and you could see the headland from that window – it's called Reenamara, by the way. Look, over there."

"Oh, yes."

"It's where you get the best lobsters. Wee Tommy fishes them out from under the rocks with a stick which has a hook on the end of it."

"You've seen this?"

"Yes. The boys and I went on a lobster hunt with the O'Friels last week. The Flynns and some others came too.

You must come with us one day next week."

"Who's Wee Tommy while he's at home or abroad?"

"He's Mr O'Friel. But nobody calls him anything except Wee Tommy – he's so small that his son Hugh could carry him for seven miles on his back without even noticing the difference."

"Hugh does this often?"

"Don't be silly!" The wife, giggling, skipped ahead at last at her own pace, jumping from one reedy tussock of grass to another over the marshy pale green patches which at dusk could be treacherous. She went on skipping until she reached the first grey slabs of rock, and then she sat down and lifted her face to the sun, eyes closed, leaning back on the palms of her hands, smiling. Just before the man reached her, he became aware that she was watching his slow progress through smiling slitted eyes, and he stumbled on one of the tussocks, misjudged the jump to the next one, and ended up cursing on the pale boggy moss, up to the tops of his socks in water. Her laugh died quickly when she saw his angry face, but he was beside her laughing at himself in a few moments.

"This was never my country," he intoned, "I was not born nor bred nor reared here and it will not have me alive nor dead. But it may well be the end of me!"

She laughed and went on laughing. "Take off your socks," she said, "and I'll hang them out of my belt to dry in the wind." She was wearing blue denims with a sort of leather scout's belt which had loops made for carrying various objects.

"They'll dry just as quickly on me, and probably much quicker," the man said.

"Wee Tommy wouldn't agree with you about ignoring wet feet. You know what he does? Before he steps out into the shallow pools at low tide he takes off his socks and puts them in his pocket. Then he rolls up his trouser legs and puts his boots back on again."

"You mean wellingtons?"

"I mean ordinary black leather boots. And he steps out

into the pool in those so that they're sopping wet by the time he's finished."

"Don't tell me. Then he takes them off and puts on his dry socks. Then he puts his boots back on, and before he's gone ten paces his socks are as wet as the boots! He could have saved himself a lot of trouble by just stepping out in the first place."

"You're wrong. The dry socks STAY dry, he says, and the boots have dried out by the time he gets home."

"Obstinate, self-deceiving peasants!" the man exploded, but good-humouredly, and he took her hand to pull her to her feet. He kept the hand in a tight grip as they walked along, as easily as though on a road because here the rocks were in flat slab formations. Small pink flowers like candytuft grew in the crevices and bent double in the sea wind. The sea itself had temporarily disappeared, though they could hear its roaring in the caves underneath.

"How was it at home when you left this morning?" the wife asked.

"All right. Mrs Cuffe says to tell you the dogs were so lonely for you that they've begun to be friendly with her and they even eat the tinned stuff occasionally."

"Poor dogs. What about you?"

"O.K. I've been messing with the sun place and you may even like it."

"What have you done?"

"Wait and see. And I let the grandchildren staying next door strip the raspberries, and then I did over the paths with sodium chlorate. Oh, and Mrs Cuffe took home some windfalls to make apple jelly."

"Did Joan ask you over to a meal as she said?"

"She did, but I managed to get out of it."

"Michael!"

"I was perfectly tactful, don't worry."

"Wait till you taste a lobster that's been only out of the tide half an hour! After weeks of basic eating you're going to enjoy this week, I can tell you. We'll probably go out with Wee Tommy again – let's see, this is Saturday. Tuesday the tide should be right again for lobsters. I'll bet he'll be going on Tuesday and we can all go with him."

"You've forgotten I don't particularly like the beasts."

"Wait till you taste one that's been crawling around the kitchen floor until the moment it's put into the boiling water!"

Cormorants screamed around their heads as they climbed the last barbed-wire fence stubbornly fixed to the bare rock. "Who," the man wanted to know, "but these land-hungry famine relicts would bother to fix a boundary to such a barrenness? Who would be likely to dispute ownership with them except these gulls?"

"If it were mine I'd do exactly the same," the wife said. "Look, this is the last stretch. Do you see where the rocks form a sort of semi-circle, like half a Greek stage? Well, that's Carraig-an-Aifrinn. It's just at the innermost point."

"Let's say we've seen it, then. Look at those clouds making straight for us." Rain clouds had clotted together beyond the next headland and were blowing lightly as the white cumulus across the dwindling stretch of the blue sky.

"It will just about catch us, if it does rain, when we've arrived at the rick and there we have shelter."

She broke away as she had done earlier and ran, beckoning him, across the bright granite, her ridged shoes gripping fast even when she leaped across the now frequent gashes in the rock face through which the sea spumed below. The man shrugged and buttoned his sheepskin higher, then followed in the same direction, though not in her footsteps. When he chose he could stride faster than she and this he did, avoiding most of the jumps by taking the long way around them, and arriving at the fan-like circle of rocks only a little after she did and only a little more breathless.

"See if you can find it," she invited, elbows leaning on a low table of rock that was not a dolmen but looked very similar. The man fancied he could actually feel the cold stone against her breasts; she could never be taught to wear enough clothes.

"You're irreverently leaning on it, of course."

"Wrong. I wouldn't." She was smiling.

The man shrugged and buttoned his collar up against the first blown drops of rain. Then he quickly stepped around her side of the rock, pulled a blue scarf out of her pocket and tied it under her chin.

"What's wrong with you is you are not safe to let out," he said, but now he was smiling. "Look, while you propose this cute game of hide-and-seek those dirty black clouds are about to disgorge their whole load on top of us."

Still smiling, the wife shook off her scarf and beckoned him. He followed, into the broken circle of rocks, some of which dripped as though the sea had somehow forced entry from below and bled through them. But when she stopped abruptly and stepped behind a mound of small rocks – like the cairn on a mountain summit – it was suddenly dry, and the limestone altar was unmistakable though much smaller than the exposed table he had seen at first. Up behind it the rock face with its savage fissures soared a hundred feet into the air so that one thought of a Gothic cathedral until one came face to face with the sky, with the one triangle of blue that remained.

"Look!" the wife said, and put a small heap of coins into his hand. He had not noticed that the altar was littered with these, sixpenny pieces and shillings of worn silver, halfpence and pence and (surely?) a couple of half-sovereigns. These were what she had put into his hand and he turned them over curiously.

"Can't understand how somebody hasn't knocked them off," he said. "How did they escape?"

"Who *would* take them? – it's a holy place."

When he turned from replacing the gold coins she was on her knees, fair head bent, but she got up almost immediately when a rainy bitter gust of wind practically took their breath away.

"I know where to go," she said, and he followed her a few yards away into a shallow cave, invisible from where they had been standing. Inside, it was dry, with a floor of small pebbles and the shells of sea-snails which, some time, might have been carried there by high tides. Pleased, he took off his sheepskin and spread it inside out on the pebbles. Suddenly he was reminded of their courtship. When she plumped down, giggling at the perfection of the shelter she had provided, he was instantly beside her, bulky and warm, breathing very fast, amorous suddenly as was his way, joking about the ghosts of the decent Mass-going peasants that were this very minute about to be startled.

The wife's quick initial response was suddenly checked, and she broke from him to sit suddenly back on her heels, cold hands cupping her knees. She saw the astonishment in his eyes and her voice did not quite register the levity she had intended.

"Perhaps we'd better make a date for same time, same place on Monday. It *ought* to have been O.K. today, but I was late, and it isn't. Unless you want twins or something by this time next year."

"Oh God, no!" At home he'd even checked the marked calendar on the inside of his wardrobe. But this was a calendar you could never quite rely on. Yet he had relied on it for the whole length of that journey. Two hundred miles had never seemed so short.

"You're not any sorrier than I am," she complained, turning away to dig into the small pebbles with her fingers.

"Sorry, yes, but you'll go on waiting for a celibate churchman in Mother Rome to change his mind again, won't you? How long is it going to take him to realise that though he may have spoken, the people of God have long since passed out of earshot?"

"I haven't and he isn't just a celibate churchman. He's the Pope."

"You haven't. And he's the Pope. And he has the right to tell you when your marriage vows made before God may be honoured and when not."

"Yes, he has the right," the wife said, on the note of stubborn finality that goes with old arguments. She was still playing with a handful of the small pebbles as he got angrily to his feet and stamped over to the mouth of the cave. For several minutes he stared out into the driving rain. Once she thought he was going to make off into it, but he came back shaking himself like a dog with something like calm restored to his face.

"Don't imagine I came all the way up here to go into all *that* again," he said.

"Monday's not really so far away," the wife placated, and he opened his mouth to reply but quickly changed his mind.

He went on to another tack. "Trouble with you is you never see beyond these desolate rainy wastes. Look at us! Huddled on a summer's day in a damp cave on the edge of the Atlantic with the rain and the furious sea thundering all around us and not even sex to keep us warm, and you think we should be happy."

"I am. And the floor of the cave is bone dry – feel!"

"Out there are sun and civilisations the sun nurtured – do you think the culture of Greece could have happened at all in a climate like this?"

"You can hardly call this place uncivilised all the same. Think of the imagination that saw this as the perfect natural place of worship that it is – and closely hidden as it had to be."

"Think of them," the man said, "struggling in their famine tatters across the rocks with the rain beating down on them, spouting their barbaric language at one another, with their fists clenched tight over the halfpence they wouldn't have been welcomed without."

"Not true. The celebrant of a Penal Mass risked death every time he celebrated it, remember. If he had to live on the halfpence of the poor, that was hardly his fault. They gave freely."

"What puzzles me is why they continued to give when the whole show was over. What's the meaning of these coins, most of which are no more than a century old. Don't tell *me* any priest couldn't bear to take the pence of the poor."

"It puzzles me too. I think maybe the money was offered up perhaps in gratitude for Emancipation or something."

"Offered to God? Money? You see, your own particular form of superstitious lunacy. Like the Thanksgiving notices you see only in Irish newspapers. 'Grateful thanks to St Anthony for great favour received.' Is the *Irish Independent* delivered by carrier pigeon to the celestial gates at ten o'clock sharp every morning? Or does St Anthony come down for a free read of the files every so often to find out who are the lousers who won't even bother to thank him?"

Now the wife was laughing too, but she stopped soon. "I'm taking you to meet Paid Eoin tonight in O'Donnell's pub," she said. "He'll tell you more than I can about this place – which, by the way, is haunted."

"We are *not* going to listen to a *sean duine liath* giving out old guff over his booze tonight?"

"Of course we are. It's great fun, and I promise you'll like him. Aren't you curious to know about who haunts Carraig-an-Aifrinn? That I do know."

"It's haunted by a pair of drunken tailors who dropped three halfpence through a slit in the rock on the way to Mass one rainy morning after Samhain. They've never given up hope of finding the money. So every night when the moon is full –"

"Keep quiet and listen. Two men and a pregnant woman came over in a curragh from the island one Sunday morning. Can you imagine landing a curragh on those rocks down there even in good weather? It seems the woman's brother was capable of handling a curragh anywhere along this coast and her husband was nearly as good. But a storm blew up suddenly – it was October – and they were drowned trying to land. They were seen in broad daylight on the edge of the crowd at Mass a short time afterwards and they still haunt these rocks."

"Very nice. Pregnant with her thirteenth child no doubt. Now come on before we hear them caterwauling – God knows, it's dark enough, though the rain seems to have stopped." He pulled her to her feet, kissed her lightly by way of peace offering, and buttoned himself back into his sheepskin. They strolled, arm in arm, back along the wet roads of rock.

"Look," said the wife, "I wouldn't doubt him. Will you look at Michael coming out to find us?"

The ten-year-old in an Aran gansy was bounding like a goat towards them over the rocks, whooping a war-cry in case they hadn't seen him. He arrived breathless but articulate. "The others are furious, Daddy, that you got away without them. I guessed where Mummy had taken you so I thought – thought I'd just meet you on the way back." He grinned, his freckled face sheepish.

"Well timed, Michael," the father applauded.

"Know what?" the boy said in his mother's ear. "Hugh's just brought in a huge salmon for Daddy's supper."

"You don't mean it?"

"Sure. And Daddy, Hugh says will you come out fishing with us in the boat on Monday?"

"I couldn't bear the cold in my aged bones."

"But Daddy, he has oilskins for us, and I was too hot out in the boat last week – even in the rain."

"Look at those other scoundrels coming out after you," the man said abruptly, and when they waved the four remote figures in blue shorts scrambled like crabs over the rocks, uttering faint aggrieved shouts as they came.

Up in the ghost village of Kilcreeshla there were hardly any lights. The green road that led to another village (now totally deserted) was invisible to all but those who knew it was there. Kilcreeshla itself had only four school-going children and as many as forty old people, so most of the stone cottages which were not abandoned were asleep early and showed no lights. Two houses built together at right angles to the road were bright, however, and bicycles leaned against the gable end. A few visitors' cars were parked together in the open flagged yard where hens picked during the daytime. When the door opened, a blast of warm talk and firelight escaped into the night air, but the man and woman who were leaving latched the door at once behind them, and only the wheeze of an old melodeon could be heard following them down the rocky overgrown road.

"We left before the fun really started," the wife protested. "You've no idea how good it gets later. Peadar hadn't even warmed up for his step dance and Paid Eoin was only on his second pint. He never begins yarning until he's well into his third one."

"Then we *did* leave at the right time," the man grinned. "You know I can't stand those whiskery ancients with their Old Moore's wisdom. You can have them all to yourself tomorrow night," he finished on a coaxing note, and then he realised he'd said more than he had intended at this juncture.

"You mean you won't come out tomorrow night?"

"I mean I won't be here tomorrow night," he said gently, an arm about her waist as he steered her down the hill to the crossroads. "I only came up to say, so to speak, that I couldn't come. I only knew I couldn't yesterday, and you were all expecting me and I thought it was better –"

"Why?"

"O'Kelly isn't satisfied with the price. I must be in town before eleven on Monday morning to see if I can push the deal through. It's possible that it may take several days. I must set off from here after lunch tomorrow."

"I mean why did you come just to say you weren't coming? That was stupid. All those preparations the O'Friels were making –"

"Stuff the O'Friels. I came to see you. Two hundred miles up here and the same back tomorrow, just to see you. I didn't like to write or telegraph."

"It would have been better."

"Look, you're not crying, are you?"

"I'm *not* crying. But you can tell Mrs O'Friel yourself – I'm not going to. I know you mentioned about this O'Kelly thing in the last letter, but I didn't think it was so important. Is it a woman?"

"Sheila, you're crazy. What the hell would I want with a woman? I've got one."

"If it is a woman, you can take her to beautiful Greece with you, for all I care. No, let me go. I'm going back to the pub, and I'll walk back later with Wee Tommy as I do every other night. Grass widowhood's nothing new to me, remember."

"Wee Tommy will be as drunk as a lord and will probably get sick all over your shoes."

"I'll risk that."

"I'm sorry. Won't you believe that I'm *sorry*."

"I believe you. Think of me on Monday night in town and I'll do you the same favour here. Goodnight. You'll be asleep by the time I get back." Her tone made it clear that this was as she wanted it to be.

Then, more quickly than he had anticipated, she twisted away from him and ran back towards the pub. He followed her slowly for a few steps, and then stopped when the blast of light and sound came again as she lifted the latch. The door closed at once, and he stood for several minutes in the darkness on the stony path, staring at the place where the light had been, listening to the wheeze of the old melodeon. Then he walked back in the direction of the crossroads, cursing softly in the silence that was only broken occasionally by the unseen incoming tide.

The Birthday Party

ON MICHAEL'S birthday Mrs Devlin arrived back from the camping site with two extra children to add to the party. The Devlins always had been a socially concerned family, but Michael thought this was going a bit far. Not that they weren't all used of course for as long as they could remember to having strangers around the house. Their special orphan was taken out from the Home on her birthday and on occasional Sundays throughout the year. At Christmas she was joined by two inmates of the old men's home down the road, and the children were told they would enjoy their own Christmas dinner all the more for sharing it. Three times every year, seasonal clothes were weeded out of the chests of drawers and made up for one or other of the travelling families at the camping site – for the past couple of years the clothes had gone to the same family, which gave Mrs Devlin more interest in gathering the bundles together since she could match clothes with children. Her own family had been inured from an early age to being separated from favourite garments since somebody else had more need of them. Successive Spanish au pair girls grew resigned to the washing and mending which preceded the making up of each parcel.

Quite suddenly, on Michael's eighth birthday, Mrs Devlin decided to take the large current bundle of summer clothes to the camping site rather than have it cluttering up the porch awaiting the day when she might be going in that direction. Everything down to the laying of the festive table was ready anyway, all the party rituals having been gone through the night before: bulky packages for Pass the Parcel had been contrived by Magdalena and Grainne, presents for the treasure hunt had been cunningly hidden by Mrs Devlin herself and the clues written. Savouries and sandwiches were made and sealed up in the larder, the cake was iced, the cocktail sausages, many dozens of them, were on order from the pork butcher. Magdalena would cook them in good time for tea, and all the smaller Devlins would vie with one another as usual to plunge in the little coloured sticks before the huge smoking dish was carried in.

It was almost lunchtime and the mountains of cocktail sausages had already been delivered when to everybody's surprise Mrs Devlin arrived back with the two travelling children who would, she said, stay on for the party. She whispered to Michael that he would enjoy his day all the more for sharing it with children who didn't even know what a birthday party was. Michael was doubtful and said so, but his mother urged him not to be selfish.

The children had to be given lunch also, of course, and places were found for them around the kitchen table. They were very clean though their clothes smelled pungently of wood smoke, and they hardly said a word. The boy had tangled red hair and was about Michael's age. His name was Corny, and his slightly younger sister was Brigid. They sat sullenly at the table, rapidly eating what was offered them as though it might be taken away if they weren't quick enough. Michael knew that he wouldn't be allowed to eat like that even on his birthday. But Mrs Devlin smiled widely at both young visitors and Mr Devlin cracked a few jokes to which only his own family responded.

Normally he didn't come home for lunch but today he had brought Michael's new bicycle in the boot of the car. Michael's thoughts were on that coveted present as he played with his food and the thoughts of everybody else were on the party, so the meal was a rushed one anyway. The guests would be arriving with their brightly wrapped offerings in not much more than an hour's time. Michael hadn't wanted a party but his mother reminded him of all the parties he had been to in the past year. Even if *he* didn't enjoy today, everybody else would. Birthdays also were for sharing, did she have to remind him?

She did. Michael was eight, but even years ago he had always considered his birthday to be a day when he should please himself. As early as five he had decided he didn't really like birthday parties except in other people's houses and he had opted for a picnic at Loughshinny instead. This was granted, so the following year they went on another picnic to the Devil's Glen. It rained heavily. His seventh birthday was decided for him and took place at the Members' Restaurant in the Zoo. Mrs Devlin had driven all the children back with her afterwards, helped by a flotilla of friends. It had worked out more expensive than a straight party and so this year they were back to custom again.

After lunch Michael went out into the avenue on his new bicycle while the remaining preparations were made. The two travelling children followed him and watched his progress under the trees with such longing that in the end he tried to teach them to ride. Brigid was quicker to catch on than her brother, but even she fell off twice and dinged the front mudguard. Michael finally left his visitors wedged against the railings outside the house while he whipped around the river walk, being careful to avoid collision with the notices saying No Cycling. When he got back, Corny and Brigid were nowhere to be seen and he rightly judged they had been called in for the party. A light summer drizzle had begun to fall and he thought his mother would make it an entirely indoor affair like Grainne's birthday in January. She hated a party that was neither one thing nor the other but meant muddy feet all over the carpets.

Inside the house he found himself bundled into a clean shirt and pants and pushed into the playroom where his brothers and sisters, the travelling children and a handful of friends were waiting uneasily around. The presents had been deposited in an old dog basket on the window seat – it was the rule that you didn't open presents until everybody had arrived because everybody had to share the pleasure. Grainne put on a record of the Boom Town Rats which she had already given Michael that morning and they all waited for the rest of the party to arrive. It was Magdalena's job to open the door and Michael's to greet everybody at the bottom of the steps outside the playroom which was just opposite the kitchen. Traditionally Mrs Devlin would appear only when it was time to open the parcels, and of course she would be in attendance for the games that always came afterwards. Then she would have a hurried meal with Michael's father in the kitchen – maybe a Spanish omelette cooked by Magdalena – and be ready to open the hall door for the parents when they came at eight o'clock to collect the children. There would be drinks laid out in the drawing-room for anybody who wanted them, but usually only a few close friends of Mr Devlin went up there.

Michael could never remember a birthday when he had actually talked to his father except that time when they had gone to the Devil's Glen. He remembered getting tired on the steep track beside the waterfall and finding himself suddenly swung up like a baby on his father's shoulders although he hadn't said a word about being tired. He even remembered what his father said, with face grinning sideways up at him and hair tickling Michael's knees. "Birthdays for me down the country were a new pair of shoes and half-a-crown – how would you have liked that, fella?" Half a crown? His father had explained about half-crowns. They were about thirteen pence. And down the country you would feel rich as a king, his father had said, with thirteen pence heavy in your pocket. Recently after the birthday parties, Michael's father would stay on and on up in the drawing-room with a few other fathers whose sons maybe had fallen asleep in the back of the car. By the time he would be free to come and talk to him, Michael himself would be in bed trying to keep awake. Recently Michael had begun to dislike the very thought of his own birthday, but he knew he mustn't be selfish.

He did like opening the parcels of course. It was a ceremony like Christmas but it was a little different this year. Mrs Devlin decided that Corny and Brigid should help with the opening. She had whispered to Michael in the hall that this would make them feel better since they hadn't brought anything, of course. Michael wasn't sure it made them feel better. They had to hand over the presents to him, after all, when they'd opened each parcel, and although Corny did this automatically, Brigid often delayed over it. Once or twice she looked as if she thought she had the right to keep the wooden jigsaw or the glider airplane or whatever for herself. Michael knew how she felt and he hoped she would be happy when she got her own wrapped-up parcel going home. His mother had spent several hours last night making up the going-home presents and he knew there would be as usual a few extra presents just in case, so Corny and Brigid could be sure of getting theirs. Michael wondered if he should tell them about the going-home presents, since they probably wouldn't know, but finally he decided a surprise would be better.

During the old familiar party games it was so hard to make them understand the routines that Mrs Devlin suggested they might like to sit and watch for a while before joining in. "My brother Ali is Dead" raised the biggest laughs as usual, but not from Corny and Brigid. During the treasure hunt the children were allowed to scatter all over the house except into Mr Devlin's study. Even the bedrooms were fair game, and because everybody enjoyed this so much Mrs Devlin thought it a special pity that Corny and Brigid couldn't play since neither of them could read. She had written the clues very simply in large block letters because not all of Michael's friends could read as well as he could, but neither Corny nor Brigid knew the alphabet. Pitying the lost look of them, she led them back to play with the presents until tea time and she gave them both a Mars bar. Since Mars bars were part of the treasure anyhow they weren't doing too badly, she told herself, but they looked lonely in the playroom all the same, considering the laughter and trampling that sounded all over the house. Corny thanked Mrs Devlin for the chocolate but his sister didn't say a word. She just bit at once into the sweet without looking up.

Around the long festive tea table there was the usual hilarity, the usual hoarding of food on their own plates by the usual children, the usual silence when the birthday candles were lit in a room dusky with the rain outside. In the candlelight nobody could have told the difference between Corny and Brigid and all the rest. Their expressions were the same as they fixed their eyes on the candles but they didn't join in the singing of "Happy birthday to you," probably Michael thought, because they didn't know the words. Only Corny joined in the clapping when Michael, with a mighty blow, quenched all the candles. Mrs Devlin decided Corny was the nicer of the two children and when he left the table before the others she took his arm and showed him where the downstairs lavatory was. He thanked her with a big smile, but when Brigid followed closely on his heels she was scowling still.

After tea however they both quite obviously enjoyed Pass the Parcel as much as anybody else and they caught quickly onto the idea. During the stampeding game of Hide and Seek which followed they made quite as much noise as anybody else, so she presumed they must be enjoying that too.

This was the stage of any party when Mrs Devlin began to long for peace and quiet and an empty house again. It was the time when she sometimes lost her temper if the children went too far. She must watch that it didn't happen this time. After the quickly snatched meal with her husband in the kitchen, which Magdalena had prepared against his arrival, things looked brighter. Magdalena had dealt very efficiently in her absence with a cut knee, an accusation of cheating, and a fight between two of the boys.

When Michael suddenly thundered into the playroom in floods of tears, it all seemed too much. He only cried harder when she shook him impatiently by the shoulders but calmed down enough to speak when his father knelt down to listen to the story which came out at last in sobbing bursts. His beautiful new bicycle was gone. There was no mistake. He'd left it against the end wall, through the side door leading to the back garden, and he'd gone to put it away when he remembered it was raining. Everybody laughed and said, Nonsense, it couldn't be gone. Somebody else must have put it away out of the rain. Michael said he'd looked everywhere, front and back, and his father said, "The rain's stopped. Let's all go and look again."

Everybody trooped out after him through the French windows but Mrs Devlin stayed behind with Magdalena, whose brown eyes were full of horror. Mrs Devlin rubbed the back of her hand across her mouth and said, "Oh God, it can't be true," but Magdalena nodded her own suspicion, then volunteered to go and look for the travelling children around the house while Mrs Devlin fetched her car keys. She had the engine already started up when the girl ran out to the front drive, shaking her head. Mrs Devlin nodded and then with set lips drove quickly down the gravelled drive onto the road. "Tell Mr Devlin I won't be long," she called out through the open window.

She knew the children couldn't be far away and they weren't. The sly little Brigid was wobbling slowly along in the direction of the main road and her brother had one hand on the bicycle carrier, jogging to keep up with her. It was mealtime in the houses round about so the quiet avenue was deserted under its laden trees. The klaxon when she blasted it practically shot both children into the air with shock. She then deliberately accelerated to scare them a bit more by driving too close, but lost sight of them for a moment before braking hard and pulling in to the kerb. Savage ungrateful little tinkers that they were, they deserved a scaring. But when she glanced into the rear mirror before slamming out of the car and running back, she couldn't see them at first, only the sadly wrecked fallen bicycle.

Was it possible they had escaped into one of the gardens? She became so convinced of this that when she did see the children at last she could hardly believe it. Brigid lay on her face very still against a brick wall, blood trickling from her head along the pavement. Corny was curled in a foetal position in the gutter, clutching one knee, and when he saw her running towards him he tried in terror to get up on what was obviously a broken leg. He fell back whining with pain, and when with heart hammering she knelt down to put her arms around him, he cowered away from her, screaming, as from somebody who intended to kill him.

He continued to scream as she went to bend over his sister who was by now lying in a widening pool of blood. Mrs Devlin didn't know how long she stood staring down at the blood and at the tangled back of the child's head. For the first time in her life she was unsure of what to do. When people began to emerge at last from the surrounding houses, drawn by the boy's continuing screams, she heard herself saying that this was what happened when a poor unfortunate child stole a bicycle she didn't know how to ride. When eventually her husband came with the local Garda sergeant, and an ambulance took the children away, she said it again, over and over again, on the way to the station: this was what happened when a poor unfortunate child stole a bicycle she didn't know how to ride.

Lord of the Back Seat

A LOVE affair with a married woman seemed, by its very nature, to promise a certain stability. It was very different from office involvements which perished quickly in the boredom of the day's comings and goings. This affair was more protected and romantic, the stuff of the very best French fiction. I had, after all, fallen in love with poor doomed Emma Bovary long before I left the small town where I grew up. Emma had simply been unfortunate in the bad egg she had chosen to love. I would never take advantage of a vulnerable woman like that. Aileen, in any case, had never even pretended to be a vulnerable woman.

She was very unlike any of the girls I knew at home or at the bank, the crudity of whose advances could never be mistaken. She wasn't, of course, a girl. She might have been thirty-six or seven when I was twenty, although I was never quite sure. One day she had been sent to me with a cheque for five hundred Deutschmarks and she wanted to know what to do with it. Could she lodge it to her account here or did she have to go to College Green and get it changed there? I told her I could change it for her, that I *was* in fact the Foreign Exchange Dept. of this small branch office. She smiled and said I didn't look like a department of any kind. When I asked her what she thought a department should look like she smiled fractionally and said "Older."

Her name was Aileen O'Malley and whether she had foreign exchange problems or not she always came to me in future. I began actually to look forward to her visits. One day, a few seconds before closing time, she rushed in with rain flowing in rivulets down a white raincoat. After I'd cashed a cheque for her she offered me a lift home with quite casual kindness. I explained that a banker has two hours work ahead of him after the public has been disposed of and she smiled regretfully. "Poor you." It was still pouring rain at five o'clock when I stood on the top step fastening up my anorak and looking down at a scene of greater traffic confusion than usual. I became aware of a klaxon blasting away in the middle of the bottleneck and there she was smiling through the open door of her car, beckoning me. I made a dash for it, through furiously hooting motorists and I brought rivers of rain into the car with me but she didn't seem to mind. "So happens I'm on my way back from delivering someone at his music lesson," she smiled. "Fortunate accident that I saw you." That was the beginning.

After she had left me a little over a year later I had grown to know her and her family so well that knowing she was gone was like losing a book you have more than half-read, whose ending you have been saving up and now will never know. It wasn't that I ever knew them individually very well, though I went to a few parties at the house, and two or three cheerful family suppers. It was that in the course of talking with her several evenings a week for long hours at a stretch, their problems had become partly mine, as I believed mine had become wholly hers. I knew which of the five children had a stammer and which used to sleepwalk to the terror of everybody whenever he was worried about school. I knew the name of each succeeding boyfriend of the charming fifteen-year-old Fiona, and I knew that the twin girls must never be separated because each complemented the other and so was miserable in her absence. Best of all, I knew Stephen, their father – his habit of shattering things by an incautious movement, his nervous cough which so irritated Aileen, his patience with the children, his occasional bouts of drunkenness. She was not, I think, a particularly good talker, yet she somehow described him so well that when I finally met him it was as though I had known him long ago except for one thing. He was much younger than I'd imagined – her own age in fact. His brown and shaggy hair gave him the look of a good-natured dog. His eyes were like that too, and I felt slightly ashamed of knowing more than I ought about him. "We lie together like two Crusaders on a tomb," she told me when I'd only known her three days. Yet five children? The youngest however was seven – the sleepwalker.

She surprised me sometimes with phrases like that. Two Crusaders on a tomb. She was not allusive as a rule and she had read no more than you would expect a girl to have read who married at twenty after a brief and I must say undistinguished career on the stage. Her largest part had been lady-in-waiting to Gertrude the Queen (no lines) but her roles became more important when she broke at last into advertising. She was, she told me, the woman whose children brought seventeen friends home to lunch because she had a habit of serving a certain brand of instant dessert on Tuesdays. She was also the girl whose change of deodorant saved her marriage. Her sense of humour, to my great joy, began to improve under my tutelage. When I first knew her she would give these facts straight, with some pride. She was particularly pleased, for instance, about that first time she wore a shawl and petticoats and was the sort of friendly Irish girl who would welcome you a hundred thousand times to a genuine Irish thatched cottage at a reasonable rent per week to include central heating. The advertisement had been shown to a club of wealthy businessmen in Dusseldorf and twice in Amsterdam. Several of our embassies had copies of it.

I can't quite remember the point at which she ceased to be a marvellous joke, not quite credible, a whim of the gods. I can remember the stage when I never did believe she would turn up next time, but that quickly passed. She rapidly became, or so I believed, essential – her too-loud laugh, her crazy optimism, the way she would fill the dingy room by the canal bridge with apples from her garden and news of her children. She would listen with absolute attention to my own bank politics, my prospects of promotion, my swollen dreams of becoming known as a poet. Best of all, she would listen when I read to her, and now and again, apart from saying, "It's lovely – I love it," she would say what was better, "I don't like the third line – it sticks out like a sore thumb, like . . ." She would then dissolve in laughter, but she would be right. I never did understand where the embryonic critical faculty came from, but it was there. It was there when she bothered to use it. It was precious because I knew nobody else to whom I could profitably read anything.

There was something else I didn't understand either and that was physical. The very first afternoon, with the rain lashing away outside and the gas fire bubbling and spluttering in my room, there was a moment of silence as she bent to take off a soaked sandal when I didn't like the freckly dimpled forearm with its golden hairs or the slightly thickened wrists. Without speaking I said No, but that became nonsense a few moments later, and remained nonsense for more than a year. Sexually she was exuberant and inventive, a little overpowering. So restless with life herself, she had lain, perhaps, too long beside her dead Crusader on his tomb, although the tomb itself was extremely comfortable. So she said. She would like to share it some time with me, she said, instead of using my two-foot-six divan with the broken spring. I assumed her to be joking.

Rainy September became a golden warm October and I wrote something which pleased me. The night I had hoped to read it to her she didn't turn up, but she rang me on a faint crackling line at ten o'clock. The weather was so lovely they had all gone down for the weekend to the cottage. This was the first I had heard of a cottage. She wanted me to take the first train down in the morning if I didn't mind using a sleeping bag and dossing down on a bunk in the boys' room.

"Even if I *had* thought of it in time you wouldn't have fitted in the car with seven of us," she laughed, and I felt this was going too far. I refused the invitation and pointed out that I would have been quite satisfied if she had just remembered to phone me to say she couldn't come that evening. There was a long surprised pause and then a gentle good-night.

I had often wondered about the type of woman who calmly incorporates a lover into the family circle (Bernard Shaw's mother was one of them) but when I met one, at last, she fitted into no category. She was certainly managing, yet resigned when firmly opposed. She was neither cold-blooded nor merely in search of convenient comfort. She seemed devoted to her family and me in apparently sensible proportions. If her husband (of whom she seemed to be quite fond) had been sexually ardent it is possible that she would never have offered me that lift home, but having done so she faced the realities of the situation in a way that was not very easy for me.

Next weekend, for instance, there was a change forecast in the weather, so she informed her husband that she would drive down alone to clean up after the summer and do some essential minor maintenance before forgetting about the cottage until next year. I accompanied her with the greatest misgivings, which proved well-founded.

The place was about seventy miles out of town, a pleasant long bungalow made of brick and cedarwood and designed, she told me, by her husband. It and an immensely ugly office block in town were the only examples of his work I ever saw; there could hardly have been less resemblance between the two. Approached by a sandy track off the road from the nearest village, the bungalow nestled without any disturbance among its sandhills. Angles of roof or gable followed the lines of the sandhills themselves, and facing it was a golden beach empty except for a few cows. They drank from a small freshwater stream which came down from the hills to end its course in the salty ocean. It was six o'clock on a Friday evening, I remember, and full tide. The water stretched calm and glittering and dark blue as far as Rosslare. The weather forecasters had evidently been mistaken. A swim seemed the most desirable thing in the world though most of the beach was in shadow.

"The water won't be cold," she promised me. "It will have soaked up all the heat of the last few weeks. You'll see."

I didn't see, but by that time it hardly mattered. I noticed that inside the house she had fingered with some surprise a bulky leather camera-case lying beside a small piece of female luggage on the kitchen table, though she made no comment when the back door leading to the beach proved to be open. I knew in my bones what we would find, and so we did. A man and a girl, both heavily tanned, lay in one another's arms against the sand dunes, in the last pool of sunshine. Aileen at once ran shouting towards them, calling impatiently to me when I held back. They were not in the least put out by the interruption – as pleased as she was it seemed to discover one another. She introduced them as Harry Lane and Sheila Meehan and me also, simply by name, without explanation. He was heavily middle-aged and swarthy, with a throaty laugh and friendly dark eyes. She seemed a mere schoolgirl, leggy and blonde and inclined to giggle.

"We had absolutely no *idea* we'd find any of you here," the girl said. "Is everybody down?"

"Only ourselves," Aileen assured them, and I intensely disliked the inclusive phrasing. It seemed that friends often used the cottage at odd times by open invitation. A second key could always be picked up from the cleaning-woman in the village. None of this I had known before, and now quite suddenly I wanted to get away.

"Excuse me, I'd like a swim before it's too cold," I said, and the girl Sheila, goose-pimply by now, snuggled up to the man and shuddered. The last medallion of sun had narrowed around them.

It was quite a few minutes later when Aileen joined me in the icy water. I was swimming by this time, not so paralysed by cold as when I had hovered for a while before plunging. Aileen waded straight out and then dived in head first as soon as she got sufficient depth. She came up beside me spluttering and breathless.

"You'll like them," she gasped. "Harry's a very clever cameraman – going to do a small job tomorrow as a matter of fact when his assistant Michael comes down with the rest of the gear."

"You *knew* this?" I asked incredulously.

"Not at all. But since I'm here and he could do with another female he's offered me a job. Said he'd be glad if you'd stand in too – already working on another composition. Will you? It can be amusing – very."

"Prostitute my person, such as it is, for a television ad? You must be crazy, Aileen."

"Don't be so stuffy." I suddenly felt years older than she was as she laughed at me before swimming powerfully away. I was happy to dog-paddle in the opposite direction. It was very cold.

It remained chilly for the evening in fact. I had expected to find the touches of domesticity painful – forgotten toys, perhaps, colouring books half-finished after some rainy day, a tweed jacket belonging to Stephen hanging up as a symbol of moral right. But it wasn't like that at all. There was hilarious joint cooking of a substantial meal, stories and jokes about people I'd never heard of, a long anecdote about the hitch they'd got to the village because Harry's car had suffered a relapse of recent engine trouble, and then a mass bundling into Aileen's station wagon for a few drinks at somebody's favourite pub. It was called The Harvester and it had a thatched roof and cartwheels outside, but inside were a ballad group from Wexford whose amplification would have been sufficient to fill the National Stadium. We went from The Harvester to a few other places similarly equipped, which left me with a screaming headache by the time we got back. Nobody had any aspirins – there was, however, an old bottle of Junior Aspirin on the bathroom shelf with one abandoned pink pill in it.

I had wondered vaguely about the mechanics of going to bed, but they proved simplicity itself. Whatever inhibitions there might have been had drowned quietly a few hours previously in the alcohol. Except mine. I was reminded of the occasions before I left home when a friend could manage to borrow his father's car and we would take out two girls to a dance twenty miles away. There was a boreen close to our town where Maurice would pull in the car on the way home. Although he would have been at a physical disadvantage in the front, it was from there the contented sounds of complete isolation always came. Lord of the back seat, I would be immobilised by embarrassment, to the amazement and sometimes annoyance of the girl.

Now in the comfortable main bedroom of the cottage it was the same. Sounds of laughter came from the other room, the scraping of something along the floor. "In there," Aileen giggled, "there are two single divans. I think they are about to be made one."

Here again was an example of her occasional felicitous turn of phrase. About to be made one.

"What's the matter, baby?" She was undressed by now, copper brown in the spill of light from the bedside lamp. She appeared to be wearing a minute white two-piece swim suit – the only two pieces of her body normally covered when she lay in the sun. The effect usually amused and touched me. I thought of them as my two pieces, but not tonight.

"I told you I have a headache," I mumbled. "A pretty lousy one, as a matter of fact."

"If only I'd been more provident," she wailed, embracing me. "What other house would you find *entirely* without aspirins? You must go to sleep my love. I'll probably waken you up in the middle of the night and your headache will be gone by then. Yes?"

"If you *can* waken me," I said sourly. She put out the light and went to open the curtains. A far brighter light from the harvest moon poured in. Glancing out, my eyes were hurt by the metallic dazzle of the sea.

"If we were swimming now," she said, "every stroke would send a shower of silver coins shooting out from our fingertips. Have you ever seen it?"

"Never."

"Some time," she smiled, and came to bed.

Scrupulously fair, she kissed me kindly and rolled away to the far edge from which in a matter of ten minutes or so I heard her quiet breathing. There was, as it happened, no moonlight awakening.

In the first daylight – cold-looking and misty now over the swinging full tide – I got up carefully and dressed. I scribbled a note explaining that after all I found I couldn't face the gregarious day. Asking her forgiveness, I signed my initial and crept away. She sighed and stirred when I opened the bedroom door but did not waken. Neither, of course, did anybody else.

It was grey and cool outside with a small breeze coming in from the sea. My headache was gone. The sense of liberation was acutely enjoyable. Somewhere a curlew cried in the distance and he was answered by another and then by a flotilla of seagulls. I turned to look at them bobbing like ducks on the full tide, swaying toy-like to and fro. The cows of yesterday had disappeared. I had a sudden impulse to swim by myself, but that would have been asking for trouble. Instead I set off down the sandy track, stopping only at a pit which had recently been dug to bury dozens of whiskey bottles. They lay like dead fish against the slope of the pit and I wondered if the grave had been left open to bury more or if Stephen had tired of the task.

Brooding about this I turned along the empty road to the village and walked at a fast clip, enjoying the crunch of my own feet in the frequent patches of gravel. When a milk lorry clattered nearby I thumbed a lift into Enniscorthy and thence by bus back to the city, still locked dustily in its Indian summer.

The relationship somehow survived this and many another setback. In the spring I had a poem published on the literary page of a Dublin newspaper and Aileen was immensely proud. Its dedication was "For A", because (and it was probably the reason for its acceptance) she had caused me to rewrite four of the lines. In the late summer I spent three moribund weeks with the maiden aunts who had reared me, and long before I went back to work I regretted refusing her invitation to spend part of the holiday at the cottage.

"How would you *explain* me to Stephen?" I had asked.

"A friend of mine *needs* no explanation," she had smiled patiently, but it hadn't seemed possible. To go swimming with the children, take part in family outings here or there, and sleep (perhaps with her occasionally when Stephen was in town) on the studio couch in a locked living-room – it didn't seem possible. When I said so she smiled impatiently this time and said how *stupid* of me. If I joined the family it would certainly not be, for the time being, as her lover but as a friend. I would sleep alone on the studio couch, or on a bunk in the boys' room, anywhere – on the beach if I liked. I thought of the cheerful young Fiona and of the possible presence of her newest boyfriend, of the discussions at night whose style would be taken from the school debating hall, the clamouring of the twins for a story, the trustful face of Ciaran the sleepwalker, and it all seemed in the most appallingly bad taste. I said so, and that evening she left early, thoughtful. I ran after her and reminded her that it was I who would suffer from her absence and she smiled but said nothing.

Almost exactly a year after the rainy September day when she had first come to the flat, I cleaned and dusted and cooked a beef Stroganoff from the Robert Carrier book I'd recently acquired. She had expressed delight at the prospect of my cooking for her. Certainly, with wine and candles and a gigantic melon marinated in brandy, all looked tempting enough, but eventually I ate alone that evening. Seven-thirty passed and eight and nine and ten, and then I sat down to the table. She had not even phoned.

The explanation when it came seemed almost adequate – an old friend of the family, Bartley, or some such name, had dropped in. He had spent ten years working on the *Toronto Globe and Mail* and now was home to stay, looking twenty years older and not ten. Fiona remembered him since the time she was a baby. There had been an impromptu celebration when he had just walked in with presents for everybody, and if she had thought I would accept she would certainly have phoned to invite me. This I knew to be true, though I don't understand why she couldn't have phoned anyway.

We somehow survived this too, though nothing was ever quite the same again. Maybe it was my fault. Resentment over the uneaten meal (to which I had never subsequently made the slightest reference) rankled for a long time. So did the fact that she no longer wanted to see me regularly. She would phone unexpectedly and say "I'm coming – O.K.?" and it was, but one could no longer look forward to the joy of seeing her on any special evening. It shouldn't particularly have mattered since I seldom went out anyhow, except now and again alone to the theatre, but it did.

Early in the new year (for whose commencement I had attended a large and cheerful party at her house) her phone calls became less and less frequent, although when we did meet everything seemed just as good as ever. She was no less ardent or attentive than she had ever been and she was even more interested in what I might have written since last time. When occasionally an evening failed it was always my fault, due to pent-up resentment and the changed pattern of our days. There was another odd thing which worried me. She never came to the bank anymore, and when I questioned her about this she passed it off lightly. It was more convenient to go to our head office since she was often in town to lunch these days. Some time or other however, she'd surprise me by just walking in. That was one promise she certainly did keep.

I think what I eventually felt most that spring, apart from the physical deprivation, was having nobody who would listen with absolute attention to the minor worries of work, the occasional sting of literary ambition, nobody in fact who would listen to anything I wanted to talk about. When I heard a promotion vacancy was about to arise in a provincial branch office I wanted to talk to her about that, but she hadn't phoned for two weeks, and then it had been only for a few minutes – chat of the children, which I was delighted to hear. But the doorbell rang (she said) before I had had a chance to say more than a few words myself, and I had to be content with the promise of an invitation to join them all for a meal soon.

Two more weeks passed. The young civil servant in the flat below asked me in for coffee one evening and in appreciation I took her to the theatre. She was twenty-two, happy, blonde and beautiful. The play was excellent. I have seldom been so bored in my life. Next evening when Aileen rang, my hand shook as I held the phone but I made myself take the initiative I had seldom taken before. I asked her to come over, mumbled something about my new-found skill in cooking, and listened in agony as the long pause lengthened to the point of incredulity that she could still be at the other end of the line.

She was. She said "I can't. Believe me it just isn't possible. It's very difficult to explain on the phone but I'm no longer free. Please try and understand!"

"You mean the stone effigy of a Crusader can suddenly sit up and join the human race again?"

"Something like that." She laughed slightly at the fact, I thought then, that I hadn't forgotten her image and then she invited me over for a meal. I said I'd come. She asked me to bring any new poems I'd written. She couldn't wait to read them.

After that happy evening, during which she shone among her own family with a kindlier light than I had ever remembered, especially when Stephen came in with a loaded briefcase and a murmured excuse, I made an appalling blunder. Loneliness, the exhilaration of watching her approve of what I had written and (once again) putting her finger on a weak line that had to go, the imagined relapse of Stephen, a painful reminder of the response of my own body to hers – what was it? What insane error of judgement caused me to write her a passionate letter next day and then post the cursed thing instead of killing it against the bars of my gas fire like all the others?

Two days later I walked home along the muddy canal banks greening already with another spring and I thought, if I stay out long enough before stepping into the dingy hall her letter will be there, crisp and blue among the circulars, the electricity bills, the postcards, the sad flotsam and jetsam of other people's lives in a big house full of small flats. But even though I lingered over a beer in Henry Grattan's pub, even though by the time I got in somebody else had laid out the afternoon's post on the hall table, there was nothing for me. There were the bills and the circulars and an airmail letter for the lovely girl in the downstairs flat and a postcard from Miami and the same crumpled grey envelope marked URGENT for the fellow who had gone away six months previously, but there was nothing for me.

It was worse on the four following days. I would come in and find my name on top of two or three pieces of post. I would carry them upstairs and leave them untouched on the table. If I didn't look before I had finished eating, before washing up, before seven o'clock, it might be there. It was not. There was a bill from the dentist, notices of preservationist activities, a letter from my aunts, a long manila envelope containing four rejected poems with his compliments from the editor of a little magazine (I had sent them to him two years ago).

Then I started wondering if she had received the letter, if I had addressed it properly, if her husband had perhaps opened it. This was the worst time of all. What I simply couldn't face then was the probability that she had received it, read it – and decided to do nothing whatever about it. I could have understood her writing a two-line reply, reproving me or expressing regret or anger or refusal to read any more letters. At this stage I would have been most grateful of all for the sort of insincerities and exaggerations often used on such occasions. I would have submitted with good grace to being told how I could never be forgotten, how nothing could ever break the bond between us. It shows I suppose what a low ebb one can sink to at such times. But I got nothing. Not a line or a phone call or any slightest acknowledgement of my sufferings.

One evening the girl downstairs asked me in to watch a play on her hired television set, and the first face I saw when I stepped into the room was Aileen's. The shock was considerable. There she was doing a young mother and daughter act with the leggy blonde girl of that horrible weekend. There was the same beach, her own bungalow in the background, a few athletic men (of whom I supposed I might have been one), an explosion of foam close to the cameras. What were they selling? – the swim suits, the beach, the oil responsible for their tanned bodies, the frozen food they would make a tasty meal out of in five minutes back at the bungalow? My cultured hostess had naturally turned down the sound and so I never learned. I closed my eyes on their fade-out smiles and didn't open them again until a mug of coffee was gently placed in my frozen hands.

It was soon after this, towards the end of March, that I phoned her one evening. Maybe blaming *her* had become so unbearable that I began for a change to blame myself. She had made her decision, told me frankly why she couldn't see me any more (what action could be more honourable than that?) and what had I done? After that letter, for God's sake, what else could she do but ignore it? There were only two replies you could make to a letter like that. She had made the tough one, as she had a perfect right to do, having decided already that the affair must end. So what? So I had to do the civilised thing and phone to apologise however difficult it might be.

It wasn't even difficult in the end. I stood uncomfortably in the draughty hall, hoping that nobody would pass in or out while I was speaking to her, and nobody did. Her voice was kind and understanding. She asked me to hold on while she carried the phone to a quieter place. Then she said she hadn't replied because she thought such insensitivity on her part would be better for me in the end. It might make me resent or hate her and hasten my recovery. She said I was twenty-two (didn't I know?) and it was such a good age. I would find somebody more worthy and also free and I would be happy. We would, she said, always be friends, always be on a special wavelength for all the rest of our lives.

After that she rang often, and chatted freely about anything and everything, especially about her family. I found myself speaking to her (often to the fury of the other residents) for as long as an hour at a time, sometimes even reading poems to her and profiting from her comments. She said she had better not ask me to the house for the moment – it would be better for me. Sometime we would meet, perhaps when I had a girl to bring with me. When I questioned her about Stephen I fancied I could see her smiling. The transformation was complete – they were very happy. He no longer brought home work and shut himself up with it late into the small hours, she said. His drinking bouts were a thing of the past, she said.

She came striding into the bank one blazing June day in a white dress which accentuated the remembered tan of last year. With her was a man of rather impressive appearance, tall, brown-skinned and silver-haired, a young-looking fifty perhaps. Together they reminded me of jet-set people in a T.V. commercial. She was cheerful and friendly as she introduced him to me, at the same time as she reached into his breast pocket for a better pen than the bank provided. He was Kevin Bartley, she said, a very old friend of the family – perhaps she had mentioned him before?

He was now home for good from Canada to settle down. He had interesting plans for his retirement, she said, including the launching of a literary magazine. At this she actually winked at me unnoticed and then smiled, as though she had just given me a secret present. Scribbling busily, she said we would all meet again soon before the summer was too advanced – as soon as she got back from Greece. Was Stephen going too? She glanced up quickly and said he unfortunately couldn't get away – much too busy at the office. I glanced routinely at her passport, slid her travellers' cheques across the counter to her and wished her a good holiday. With difficulty I suppressed an impulse to wish them both a good holiday.

When they had gone I went to the coffee room but couldn't hold the cup for the shaking of my hands. I remembered now when I had first heard about this Kevin Bartley, the night I'd cooked the meal and she hadn't come becausc some old friend had just walked in out of the blue – wasn't that it? Quite soon afterwards the dead Crusader had sat up suddenly in his tomb. Why hadn't I realised that the dead don't rise again, not in this life?

It was high summer when I left Dublin. The provincial town of my promotion was almost identical with the one of my birth – a tree-lined mall, seventeen pubs, an air of kindly and resigned stagnation. I welcomed it as eagerly as five years previously I had welcomed escape from all this to the capital. I had said in that unforgotten letter (fully believing it to be true), "I carry you hidden in my bloodstream like some virus awaiting its time and you will never go away," but it wasn't quite true. Physically she did go away so positively that at times I had to remind myself why there was nothing I now wanted to do, nobody I wanted to see. The people who did not go away (and who are with me still) are her children whom I hardly knew at all and her husband whom I feel at last I know only too well.

An Idle Woman

THE lawn was just beginning to be untidy, an autumn happening which each year took Joanna by surprise. As soon as you picked the early tree, many of its leaves came down with the small russet apples and lay in a circle on the neat lawn, neater than usual because of the boys' long absence with their grandparents. Then a single wild night would bring a scattering of leaves from the other trees, although the late apples held fast.

On the day Doyle came, there would be a magical transformation. There would be a green illusion of early summer again, and not a leaf to be seen on the lawn until the next wild night. Doyle would come tomorrow, so what use to sweep? Instead, wandering into the apple house, from which she could hear the phone if it rang in the kitchen, Joanna began to arrange the apples on a top shelf. She had to stretch up on her toes to do this, but it was the usual place for good eaters. Cooking apples were stored within reach of small fingers because it didn't matter about them. However many boys came to play, nobody would bother taking home cooking apples. One year she had found the precious russets being carried off the shelves in paper bags supplied by young Adrian himself. They were going to neighbouring houses where there was already a glut of garden fruit. After this, Brendan suggested using the highest shelves for all eaters. She or he would have to fetch fruit for the house whenever it was necessary, but at least they knew it would be there.

Calf muscles aching a bit from the stretch, she wandered out into the sun again, having put away two chips of apples. There was one chip left but that could wait until tomorrow. Before going down the garden to the sunniest place, she looked in through the kitchen window at the white phone, silent in its cradle, and willed it to ring. It did not. Sighing, and with a shrug, she strolled on down the garden.

Michael would not phone now. This was the time the afternoon post had to be gone through with his secretary, just as in her husband's office. The offices, in fact, were on opposite sides of the same Georgian street, and Brendan very often went to the Saddle Room for lunch with Michael. What did they talk about? If she asked Brendan, even in bed, he would just say he didn't remember, and it would probably be true, but some time she would have to ask Michael: "I don't suppose either of you would ever bother to talk about me?"

Flopping into a deckchair in a hot part of the garden, she lowered her eyes and looked into his, smiling, always a little evasive, blinking at her behind dark-rimmed spectacles which magnified the upturned black lashes and strengthened the summer blue of his eyes. Spectacles off, his lashes were shorter but just as thick, and the eyes themselves were paler. It was only last night that she had seen him without spectacles for the first time. Without spectacles, then without shirt and trousers, without anything at all. His body was not white, though he seldom lay in the sun, but golden in the smoky light of the oil lamp in his bedroom. He was perhaps a little taller than Brendan, with soft cushions of flesh where Brendan was bony.

It had been June, when the boys first went away, that she had suddenly become physically aware of him, of his patient closed face and the spectacled eyes watching her as she laid out tea in the garden. Brendan had brought him home from the office and she had tried to make him take off his jacket to relax in the sun. He had shaken his head and crossed his legs and settled back smiling, in the deckchair. He had asked her, as always, about the children, what news there was of each.

And then later, as he watched her busy about the meal, she was sharply conscious for the first time of every breath he drew, of his aloneness, of the trendy Georgian mews where there was nobody waiting any more when he got home. He would wash up the breakfast things and set his meal for the next morning, pick up a book and leave it down, maybe switch on the late news, and then go to bed entirely alone, as he had done for all of five years.

Shivering, she gathered up her things and went back along the winding path to the house. Brendan would bring in the deckchairs as he always did. She heard his key in the lock as she banged the back door and stepped into the blinding darkness of indoors. Almost immediately the telephone shrilled out. She ran down the steps into the kitchen, raced across the tiles, but the phone went dead just as she picked it up. Almost immediately it rang again. Wrong number.

Over breakfast next morning, Brendan put down his paper and studied her. "Are you by any chance missing the lads? You seem a bit downhearted these days."

"I am missing them, of course – the unnatural quiet. But you've no idea how much more I can get done."

"How much more of what?" He was smiling but she could detect no malice in the question. "What I was thinking was that we might take a trip home to Galway at the weekend and see the boys, see everybody. It would make a break, wouldn't it?"

Her heart began to race in alarm but he didn't notice. "It would be lovely. But have you forgotten we're having the Dillons for a meal on Saturday? It was put off from a fortnight ago when Liam had that throat thing. I've asked Maire too to take the bare look off the four of us."

"You could put them off again."

"I wouldn't like to do that," she said, "I had even thought of ringing Michael to make up a sixth."

"Very well," Brendan said. He rose to go, disappointed but not, she could see, angry. He looked at her closely before kissing her with the sort of paternal affection she sometimes felt it would be better to accept instead of resent.

When the time came to give Doyle his cup of tea, she still

had not decided to phone. Three calls had come in, and three times she had composed herself to hear his voice. She was thirty-six hours away from him, and from the smoky oil lamp, but she had never really left his room. When Doyle made his offerings of local gossip – they shared him with six of their neighbours – she tried to listen but could not have repeated a single item of news once he was back down there clipping edges at the bottom of the garden.

Now there was no reason not to phone, and she had, after all, a reason. The invitation to join them on Saturday was no different from a dozen others. But *he* had said he would ring. It had never occurred to her that he would not phone next day (as Brendan had done so long before their marriage every single morning whether he had anything to say or not). She would wait until this afternoon, and by then Michael would surely have thought of her and picked up the phone.

In the afternoon, which was hot and still, Doyle was out working in the front of the house. Even if he heard the phone he would never answer it, and if she took a book down to her usual place for sunbathing she would hear nothing. Suddenly angry at her new feeling of dependence, she carried the phone into Brendan's bright den on the first landing and plugged it in.

At the desk she fiddled before dialling and then dialled the number very quickly. His secretary asked her to hold on. Was it a personal call, she came back to ask. Finally she heard Michael's voice, very soft, like Brendan's because they had grown up within ten miles of one another in the same countryside. He sounded abstracted – yet it couldn't be his really busy time yet. Too soon after lunch. Yes, he was well, and how was she? No, Saturday was impossible because he was going down to his parents for the weekend. But he would be in touch. Would he ring her, she heard herself asking, when he got back on Monday? He wasn't sure if that would be possible, but of course he would be in touch. Goodbye, thanks for the invitation, and that was that.

She wanted to get out of the house then, anywhere, and she left a note for Brendan. "So hot that I have to get out for a swim. Will you be an angel and pay off Doyle? Love, J." She changed quickly into a swimsuit and dressed again over it.

Inside the car it was hot as a greenhouse, so she opened all the windows before starting up the engine. Because of the weather she was sure that all the nearby places where she usually went swimming would be crowded. The bulk of the British holidaymakers would be gone, but the beaches would still be crowded with family parties, with basking schoolchildren, with old men who had always lived by the sea and who had wrinkled coppery bodies from which the tan never faded. She knew of at least six of those who lay on the rocks like illustrations of Indian famine, eyes closed in simian brown faces, slack chins lifted to the last warmth of life.

She could not imagine why she should carry the images of these old men with her as she headed away from them into the mountains. Up there the blue empty spaces only filled up at weekends. Even the road out through Rathfarnham was empty, except for the rising dust after weeks of drought.

The strong draught of wind which lifted her hair became too much as the car climbed higher and she stopped to close the window on one side. On an impulse she stepped out into the dusty road and looked along the blackberry hedges for some sign of ripeness. Most of the berries were bright red still, some green. Anyhow they would have to wait until the boys came home. Picking blackberries was a ritual with rules and conventions and one did not do it in their absence.

She found a ripe one and put it in her mouth, and as the juice spurted, she found she was crying. The tears stung her eyelids before spilling over and down but she didn't care. What had made her think he might be serious? Men in his position were not, she supposed, accustomed to refuse what was freely offered, so what cause for complaint could she have? She deliberately recalled the night before last again, the beginning of it all, only forty-eight hours ago. He had said, "Don't go away, to let me think about it. If I think about it, I shall say no, Joanna, so don't go away from me." He took off his heavy spectacles, laid them on a bookshelf, smiled at her with the undefended eyes, and took her hand. Without touching her, except for the hand, he led her up the shallow flight of stairs to the panelled room where the oil lamp was. There was some light from a street lamp in the cobbled laneway outside, and that was all until the flame leaped and bubbled in the pink glass globe. Carefully he regulated it, and she could still smell the incense tang of the oil moistening an old wick as the flame steadied and climbed. After he had drawn the curtains, he had said, "You are beautiful. Did you know that?"

She shook her head several times and stepped back into the car. Shoulders and head up, she drove very fast up into the skyline to Sally Gap. Up there was a cold wind that made her realise summer was already gone; the bracken was a brownish haze along the ridges of the Featherbed, and up on the telegraph wires swallows were gathering. But when she began to drop down into the glen, summer reasserted itself in the softening air, in the hum of the insects, when she stepped out of the car at McGuirk's, in the scent of hedge roses and the drone of bees in the cottage garden.

She took the path winding through heather to the lake, and in the shadow of the hills it was inkily black, not blue as she had imagined it. At the shingly edges the water was the colour of cider and the small pebbles were gold. Still, she had come for a swim, so she peeled off her clothes down to the swimming togs and waded in, chilled to the bone.

Quite suddenly the shingle shelved under her feet and she was adrift in icy deep water. She struck out strongly and kept swimming until she didn't feel cold any more. Then she turned over on her back and opened her eyes on a separate universe of blue, or rather on so many layers of blue that she began to turn her head and blink, measuring them. The water brimmed and hummed in her ears and her hair floated free like seaweed. Long waves of remembered pleasure flowed through her, and she felt almost happy.

An hour later, as she drove in through the gates at home, she didn't feel anything except tired and vaguely peaceful. A decision had anyhow been reached, and she went to find Brendan. He was seated by the lamp in the living-room, mending a leather schoolbag and listening to chamber music. On his finger was one of her thimbles, too small, but apparently usable. She noticed that as usual he had acquired the right material for a particular job. She would have made do with button thread, but his thread was strong and waxed, almost like a fishing line. He groaned as he looked up at her.

"Why aren't your fingers bigger, so that I can use your thimbles? Three times this one has bounced off, and look at my finger."

She bent to lick away the blood. "Poor Brendan, did you have something to eat?"

"No, I decided to wait for you. I'll cook us an omelette when I've finished this."

"Look, I won't be long getting a meal together because I'm starving myself anyhow after that swim. See you in a few minutes."

She left him to his patient, slow stitching and his Beethoven quartet, and in the kitchen she prepared a cheese souffle. When it was in the oven, she went back into the living-room once more.

"I've been thinking about the weekend," she said carefully, "and, you know, it seems a pity to spoil your idea just because of Saturday. I'll phone them all and put them off until next Saturday. It's not too far away."

"Splendid," he said. "If this weather holds you're going to enjoy it. You haven't been swimming in the Atlantic yet this year, remember."

"But how about you?"

"Well, of course, I'll probably enjoy it too," he conceded.

This was typical of him. He did things for her, including occasional lovemaking, out of a sense of duty, just as he did things for the children, and he even liked to make this clear. Asking him if he enjoyed such activities was in a way a sort of impertinence. Did a father enjoy taking his children to the Zoo or to see Santa Claus?

"By the way," he said after a slight pause, "do you think it might be a good idea to bring the boys back with us now instead of calling for them later as planned? There's only ten days left of the holiday anyhow."

"No, I don't think it would be a good idea," she said rather too quickly. "Gran and Granpa would be very disappointed – you know they would. And the boys might as well have the advantage of the lovely weather. And won't it be a good excuse for us to go down next weekend?"

"What about the dinner party?" he asked quietly, and she blushed.

"Of course – I'm an idiot. Look, we'll have a *really* early start on Sunday and make it there and back in one day. Isn't that the best idea?"

"I suppose so." He was engrossed again in his job, so she went back to look at the oven, wondering at her own lack of self-possession. Luckily Brendan wasn't the sort to notice.

Friday morning passed slowly because the cleaning woman came, so there wasn't much for Joanna to do. Normally she would go out, but instead she decided to stay with a book in the garden, and instructed Mrs Collins to let her know if there were any telephone calls. There were two – the second in the soft blurry voice she had been expecting. But it was only Brendan to tell her to have the bag packed by three as he would be ready to set off by then – was that O.K. for her?

O.K. for her. Her hand stayed on the receiver after she had put it back and, with distaste, she watched it trembling. She hoped he would telephone after three this afternoon and listen to the phone clamouring through the empty house and feel disappointed and lost as she did now.

But of course it wouldn't be like that at all. His secretary would phone, if anybody did. She would listen indifferently to the unheeded bell and simply say, "Sorry, Mr Warren, Mrs Carroll doesn't seem to be available. Shall I try again later?"

Don't bother, Michael – oh, why should you bother to try again later? It's only the fourth day, tonight will be only the fourth night, and maybe you won't feel like it again for a week or so. So why bother about *me*?

On Saturday morning in Galway Brendan disappeared into a doorway on Shop Street and emerged with a gold Claddagh ring. "We can change it if it doesn't fit, but I bet you five pence it will," he said happily, and it did, perfectly. She handed over five pence and kissed him there in the street, and then they went to pick up the boys at the barber's. He had said that the ring was an unbirthday present, but she knew why he had given it to her. It was because last night, in his parents' house, in the room where he had grown up and built cars and toy planes and done his homework, she had turned away in tears when he tried to make love to her for the first time in six weeks. He wanted to show that he didn't hold it against her.

On Sunday, the sixth day, he came swimming with her and the boys in the rough Atlantic swell. It was three years since he had had a swim anywhere except in the Mediterranean, and he shivered for an hour afterwards. The boys called him "poor ancient Father William" and brought him the car rug which he gratefully draped around his shoulders in an attempt to warm himself.

That evening, home again after the long drive away from the setting sun, he said to her, "Go and pour us a drink, love, and I'll get the supper." He carved a cold chicken given them by his mother, and garnished it with a green salad reeking with too much garlic. She laughed at him and told him he must only rub the bowl with a freshly cut clove of garlic – just rub it over, no more.

"Next time I'll remember," he said, but there was amusement in his eyes as he poured the wine for her. The bottle of white Burgundy had lain with a red one on a back shelf of the larder after a party in May. She had forgotten they had wine in the house; he had remembered in time to chill it slightly, and it was delicious.

"Are we," she said, commenting on its goodness, "celebrating something?"

"It's too soon to say," he smiled, "although I might be celebrating my return alive from the Atlantic this morning."

"You did seem to be frozen," she agreed, breaking bread and crumbling it absentmindedly. Bitterly she regretted having asked for that telephone call – she hadn't even decided on it, there was no reason. Suddenly she had heard herself saying it, that was all. His answer had made it quite clear that he wouldn't phone, and that was why she had an angry knot in her throat just now. Not tears. Not tears any more.

"Listen, Joanna," Brendan cut in gently, a hand covering hers on the table, "do you want to discuss it? Could you?"

Startled, she blinked, took a sip of wine, and looked at him. There was that look on his face that was the same as when the children had needed to be picked up and comforted, bandaged or cleaned up. She didn't look away, but neither did she speak because the suspicion of his knowing was so bewildering.

"Have some more wine," he urged, and when she nodded he filled up the glass to the brim before putting a token splash into his own.

"I don't think I could talk about anything important now," she said at last.

"Please try," he said. "I'd like to take that look of the end of the world off your face because it has been worrying me all the week. Look at me Joanna." He hadn't combed his hair since the drive home, and it was scattered like a terrier's across his brow and into his eyes. When it was smooth it was very blond; now it was dark and almost reddish in the direct spill of light from the table-lamp.

His eyes still had the compassionate look she had first noticed with the children. "Do you think you will feel better or worse if you tell me?" She sighed and looked down at her plate, wondering what he imagined might be the matter with her.

"All right then," he threatened, tightening his hand on hers, "if you don't tell me tomorrow, I'll tell *you*."

Next morning when she took in the post before Brendan had come down, she stood in the hall staring in disbelief at one of the envelopes. Surely it was Michael's hand – but it was addressed to Brendan, not to her. Not even to both of them. Just to Brendan.

She put it at the bottom of the heap and left it beside Brendan's cup at the breakfast table, and she tried to be casual when he came down glossy and burnished and wearing a clean white shirt. He kissed the top of her head and then applied himself to his breakfast and his letters.

As she had feared, he did not open each as it came. He flicked through them murmuring, "Bill. Invitation. Receipt. Aunt Bernadette again. Ah." Her blood raced as he took up Michael's letter and, unable to watch while he opened it, she went across to the oven. He made slightly surprised musing sounds as he read, and when, weak-kneed, she sat down again, he passed the letter across to her.

> My dear Brendan,
>
> I wonder would you find time to look in on Monday afternoon when I shall be back in town and greatly in need of your help in the handling of Mr K? You'll remember his history – indeed I've more than once been grateful for your fresh look at the whole monumental problem of that family. Maybe if you told Joanna some of the facts, her advice might be of the greatest significance in relation to the question of that unlucky stepdaughter Emily. I have two further papers I'd like your opinion on, by the way. Any time after 3 o'clock would suit me very well. Some evening you and Joanna and I must all get together for a meal – à bientôt, then, Michael.

"Monday," Brendan said. "That's today."

Quite suddenly, tears poured uncontrollably from her

eyes and she hurried from the table, grateful that he did not make any attempt to follow her. Up in their bedroom she flung herself on the low divan and wept like a child, her face pressed into the pervasive fluff of the cotton bedspread.

Clearly, despite her lyrical memories, he must have been disappointed by Tuesday's events. He must have decided that the game wasn't worth the candle and that the best thing was to pretend that nothing had happened at all. How could he do this? How treat with cool and casual friendship somebody who for five hours of one evening had been part of him so that she fancied by stretching out the fingers of one hand she could make his move simultaneously.

Practically suffocated by the tufted white cotton, she found herself remembering in detail his caresses. Brendan and she were the same age but his lovemaking was like everything else he did, paternal. It was patient and studied and sometimes even successful, but she could not believe he ever gave himself up wholly to something so trivial, so transient. This, she imagined him saying to himself, is how the sweet creatures are made and one must go along with them. It keeps them happy.

But Michael, your compulsive needs and your tears, and hour melting into hour. Nothing, it meant nothing, and for all I know I was wrong in believing him always alone since Ruth died. I may be one of half a dozen women willing to jump into his bed whenever he has need of them.

This at least she knew to be nonsense, and she sat up to dry her eyes. Far away, she heard a door banging and knew that Brendan had left for work. She felt grateful to him for not trying to talk to her. She felt equally grateful when he rang at midday, even though the sound of the telephone made her leap unnecessarily once again.

He wanted her to meet him in town for lunch and they would go to a new place. She knew this new place by repute. He and Michael sometimes met there.

"I'd prefer it," she said, "if you came home. Could you? – just for today?"

"See you in less than an hour," he said.

He was casual over the meal and disinclined to question her. He told her the latest about a few cases with which she was already familiar, and they laughed over the tenth will in eighteen months of Eveline Jackson O'Dowd, spinster of this city. Her long-suffering nephew was again left out in the cold with a mere £200. They took their coffee out into the garden, where he sat in the shade of the clematis and she sat in the sun, her face lifted up after two sips of coffee and her eyes closed, although she was still smiling over Eveline Jackson O'Dowd.

"Talk to me," he said, "if you can, and I'll listen. Tell me everything that's bothering you. If you won't, I'll tell you."

"Tell me, then," she heard herself saying.

"You mustn't expect too much of him, Jo." The voice was gentle and she didn't open her eyes. "Remember that Michael and I have been friends since we both went up to Jarlath's when we were eleven years old, two raw country lads from the back of beyond among the gentlemen sons of grocers and publicans. He can't cope with this situation because he has no guidelines to follow."

"What situation?" she said, knowing it was ridiculous.

His laugh reproved her, but very gently, before he went on. "He allowed himself to be moved by you in a way that was completely out of character for him, and he simply doesn't know how to handle this. He's a quite simple person really, despite the surface polish, not a vile seducer by nature, not a lover of other men's wives, particularly mine. If one asked him how it had happened, he wouldn't know."

"You're wrong, because although you seem to know most things, you don't know everything. He didn't invite me to the house. I just went. It was during that evening when you were playing the round with Tom and I didn't want to watch. I went to him because he was the one person in the world who *needed* me at that very moment. He had never expressed his need, but that didn't matter. I had felt it most of the summer – ever since June."

"Look Joanna, you wouldn't admit it, but you've been lonely without the boys and I've been an insensitive clod about everything. True, I didn't see how I could get away again this summer when we'd taken that holiday in May, but I shouldn't have left you with so much time on your hands."

"Don't be so humble!" she said angrily, getting up and walking around. "Would any other man blame himself when his wife takes a lover?"

"Remember the Victorian grandmother's guideline for young brides," Brendan smiled. "If he drinks, it's her fault; if she's unfaithful, it's his." He stretched out his hand to her, unwilling to step into the sun for even a moment from his screen of clematis. Hair and skin equally fair, he never had taken any chances with the sun. She looked now at his protected fairness with a sort of distaste.

Even in Spain, he had lain every afternoon with his books sprawled in the shade of the terrace while she went back to the beach. He would come in the early morning, and stay until nearly eleven, but after that he never stirred out until late evening. However, she took the offered hand and sat down on the rug at his feet.

"You're beautiful," he said unexpectedly. "Why should I blame him?"

That struck her as so amusing that she laughed softly, and as soon as she did, she felt momentarily cheered, even a little playful.

"You should blame him for making me miserable," she said. "This is the seventh day and he hasn't even phoned. I might be dead for all he cares. If the positions were reversed, *you* wouldn't do that."

"I might too," Brendan said, "if I absolutely couldn't think out my next move. First of all he's surprised, possibly even shocked at himself for – as he would probably see it now – taking advantage of you. Remember that Ruth is five years dead, after only three years of marriage, and I swear that this is the first time since that he has touched a woman. You've often said yourself how solitary he is, and it can't be that he hasn't had opportunities. He's quite," and she was amused again by his cough, "presentable, I suppose, and then he has that tragic air that I presume women find attractive. But the point is, until now, nobody has attracted him, and he is most likely appalled that when it did happen it should have been you."

She heard the words again as clearly as when he had spoken them to her: "Don't go away, to let me think about it. If I think about it I shall say no, so don't go away from me."

Brendan said, "Can't you understand, love, that he knows he has behaved like a bastard and he can see no future in the happiness he must have found with you, so he distrusts it. He doesn't know what to do, so he does nothing at all."

"He didn't have to write that silly letter," she said, injured again when she thought about it.

"That was a childish effort on his part to pretend that nothing had happened – and especially to pretend to *me* that nothing had happened, so that in the end nobody might be hurt."

"If you think that, you don't know me, or the strength of the feelings he aroused in me and has been arousing for a long time."

"Maybe, but he can't be sure of that. And I know it's largely my fault because I've been neglecting you."

"You must go back now or you won't be in time to go and see him," she said.

"This is much more important than going to see him," Brendan said. "In fact, I am not going to see him this afternoon. Excuse me a minute." Slowly, as he did everything, he got up and walked back along the path to the house. She rolled the rug out into the sun and lay on it, listening to a very small dry wind among the crab apples and marvelling at the continued blast of heat from the autumn sun. But this was earlier in the afternoon than she was usually out here. Soon the shadows would gather, two hours earlier than in June, and it would be cold.

He came back, carrying more coffee on a tray, and he had iced hers. Touched at this, she accepted the cup, smiling.

"What did you say?"

"Just left a message with Miss Murphy that I'd phone and see him some other day. Push over there."

Surprised, she saw him drop onto the rug beside her, then stretch out on one elbow. Usually he never sat down except on a chair, hated the beach and hated meals in the garden.

"Do you remember Ruth very well?" he asked unexpectedly.

"Well enough, I suppose. I never thought her nice enough for Michael, to tell you the truth. When people are dead you usually only remember the good things about them. But I remember how close together Ruth's eyes were and how she watched people when they weren't looking and what a loud voice she had although she was so small. And I can remember how often she contradicted him in public."

"He was crazy about her all the same," Brendan said. "She refused to marry him four times and he went on asking her. Don't make any mistake about it, they were very happy. And remember, after two misses she insisted on trying for the third time almost at once because she could see how crazy Michael was about our kids. She was advised against it, but she wouldn't listen. That's what shattered Michael, you see. He feels that in a way he killed her."

"I never thought of it that way," she said.

"I know, because of the hours and hours he talked to me about it after she died. He blames himself for not actually pretending that he disliked children and didn't want any. You know, around that time, he not only almost ran his own practice into the ground, but mine as well. He talked to me for most of every afternoon for a year after Ruth died. I never told you because it seemed too terrible and too private and I saw no reason to worry you anyway."

"Oh, Michael," she said, "poor, poor Michael."

"If you want to know, I think this is probably a very good sign. In all modesty, I think I kept him alive by just listening to him that first year. You have probably unfrozen him sexually now. He's the sort of man who needs to marry again, and this is probably the first step towards it."

"I don't think Michael's at all the sort of man who would marry again," she said in a low voice. "Besides, I'm not sure I'm not in love with him."

"Are you? Or is it largely pity? And anyhow, even if you are, does that mean you wouldn't allow him to re-marry?"

"Don't be silly. As though I could prevent him!"

"Let's wait and see, anyhow, Joanna." His eyes were gently mocking her.

"How do you mean?"

"Let's see him normally just as usual, just as he suggests. Wait until he makes the first approach to you before you do anything about seeing him alone. The thing is, I'm prepared to help him as far as necessary, but I'm not prepared to have you hurt in the process. On the other hand, if you do want him, I'm prepared to wait until it wears off."

He rolled over and took her in his arms, smiling, the sun in his pale eyes. His concern for her was suddenly comforting. For all he had said in Michael's defence, Michael was, after all, only prepared to let her suffer in the interests of his own conscience. Brendan was prepared to let her have a lover if that was what she wanted.

Was it in fact what she wanted? She looked into the pale smiling eyes for some sign of strong feeling, but she found none. No trace of normal jealousy and, although he had called her beautiful, not the least tension of desire. How long was it, in fact, since he had really needed to touch her? His arms were companionably around her, and she rolled free, suddenly back in the panelled oak bedroom, smelling the wick of the oil lamp.

"All right," she agreed, "let's wait and see." Waiting and seeing suited her very well because she believed she knew how far away she was from any real decision.

Next morning, the eighth day, at the breakfast table, she understood properly for the first time why Michael had not phoned, and she felt liberated as after an illness.

"I suppose," Brendan said, getting up, "you wouldn't like to come in and have lunch with me in town today? We might drop in later on Michael and tell him we'll take him up on that offer."

"I'd love to have lunch with you," she said, smiling at the anxiety on his face. As he was crossing the kitchen floor the telephone rang and she smiled at him again.

"You take it?" she queried.

"No. You know it *is* for you at last?"

"Probably," she said, and then, smiling across at him, "See you at one o'clock in the office."

Although she was impatient to lift the phone, it was suddenly very important to be gentle, as she knew he would never fail to be with her in any circumstances whatever.

The Zoological Gardens

DELIA had reckoned without the thickness of the fog. She had no sooner left the immediate surroundings of the tramline before she realised she had no idea which way she was facing, no idea even whereabouts the step from pavement to road might be. Because the swirling woolly dampness disturbed her she closed her eyes for a moment and stood quite still, trying to imagine the wide steep canal bridge with its wet cobblestones or the steps which ought to be to the left of the bus stop. Down those steps was the row of little red-bricks where she and her mother had lived alone since the family scattered. In the foggy darkness when the last tram had sailed away, she felt her mother's fingers tighten on her arm. "Are you still awake, Delia?" The voice was querulous as in life.

She opened her eyes again and shook her head, still not able to decide which way she should turn. She hadn't known a fog like this since she was a child. She remembered her father coming in with the dog, saying only for that bowler, he'd never have got home from Scully's pub. Dogs were quare ones, her father chuckled. They had some way of navigating that human beings had forgotten. Good oul' Prince. The dog's coat was beaded with damp and his wet tail slapped her legs. The damp stood up in little bubbles on her father's coat too, and he took her by the hand to show her how you couldn't even see the front gate, so thick was the fog. In London, her father said, they called a fog like that a pea-souper. Her mother shouted to them to come in out of that before they got their death of cold but her father had hoisted her up in his arms, swinging her a bit against his cold damp coat before bringing her in. She felt glad she didn't have to go out in that fog, but if she did ever have to go out in a fog like that, she knew she'd like her father to be with her. And Prince too, of course.

Telling herself she couldn't stand here in the wet all night, she took a few steps in one direction and then, hopelessly, in another, frightened as much by the silence as by the hollow sounds of people's feet she couldn't see. She held up one hand in front of her face and almost panicked when she couldn't see that either, but she told herself this was ridiculous. She could have stayed the night with the Cronins where she always went to tea on Tuesdays, but she'd refused. Her home was only a tram-ride away. She never liked to waken up away from her own place even though her mother was dead this four years and there was no reason why she shouldn't stay over any time she liked. She supposed it was what you were used to. But she didn't like the thought of using other people's beds, other people's towels, or especially sitting down to breakfast at any other table than the one in her own kitchen facing the canal banks where sometimes the seagulls would be screeching around and even now and again come to her window for food. Her mother had called them dirty scavengers but Delia liked the big white drifting bodies and the huge spread of their wings because they reminded her of the sea and those picnics in Dollymount with her cousins long ago.

The thought of the canal frightened her all over again. Suppose she walked into it? As easily as you'd step off a pavement? Once she had seen what two days in the water had done to a poor woman who fell in the worse for drink. Anybody could fall in drunk or sober tonight. A man at the seventh lock had brought her over to see this big pale thing caught among the weeds and the newspapers and the cigarette wrappers. Molly Dunne, a poor creature who would beg for drink money if she couldn't get it any other way. When you were lonely drink must be a comfort but it was a dangerous comfort she wouldn't tamper with herself. Going for a walk with the dog was a good thing if you were lonely, especially along by the canal where other people came to walk their dogs. People with dogs were always easier to talk to, and usually all you had to do was ask the dog's name and they told you all about him. Then you in turn could tell them about Prince, about all the dogs called Prince you'd kept since you were a child, most of them black and white and friendly and with a touch of the collie in them. She wished Prince would run up to her now, his tail thumping the ground, but it was a bit late. Prince would most likely be curled up in the porch waiting for her to come in, exhausted after his day's rooting along the canal. When he was a young dog he used to carry up the dead rats in his mouth and leave them in front of the back door for her to praise him but he was too old for that sort of caper now. Sometimes she felt too old herself to start off with another young dog if anything happened to Prince, but all the same she didn't see how she could do without a dog after all these years. Not unless she got married, but that was a foolish thought. She'd promised her mother she'd never get married so long as God spared her a mother, and God had spared her a mother well into the old lady's eightieth year. A fine long life she had had, and who would grudge it to her even if she was a shade cross from time to time with the rheumatics. And she wasn't like some, leaving every penny she had for masses in Mount Argus. She'd left the house and everything else she had to Delia just as she'd always said she would, so who could complain? Danny in America could, and he was quick to point out that he as the eldest son had a better right to his mother's property than Delia, but she had taken the advice of her friends the Cronins and paid no heed to him. There was the will with the solicitor to show who had the best right to the house, so what could Danny or anybody else do? She'd never heard from him again although all the boys used to write at Christmas while the old lady was alive. Some of them even sent lovely coloured pictures of their children and even of the big ones wearing cap and gown. Those pictures were still on the top of the piano in the front room, and they made work twice a week when she did the dusting, but it was lovely to have them all the same.

She jumped and almost cried out when a hand touched her arm and a kind voice said, "Could I help you at all? I have a class of X-ray eyes!"

He had a nice friendly voice, but she couldn't see his face, or his eyes, just a dark outline in the fog. She knew it must be coming up to twelve o'clock and he might be up to no good, but if he could see in the fog, as he said, he might get her home. She had almost decided to trust her instinct that he was genuinely helpful when he spoke again.

"Would I be right in thinking you don't live too far away? Haven't I seen you sometimes out for a walk with a black and white dog?"

"Indeed and I'm sure you have. Prince brings me out for a walk every day." He responded well to the old joke and she liked his laugh too. He was all right. "I live in number seven Albert Terrace. Just down the steps, if I could only see them," she said.

"No bother," he said easily. "You're turned the wrong way. You were walking away from home. Isn't the fog a terror?"

"I don't remember it so bad since I was a young one," Delia said. "It would nearly frighten you."

"It's lifting a bit," her companion said cheerfully, "I'd say it will be clear by morning. Mind the steps now." Very gently he guided her, his hand on her arm hardly felt.

As they walked along the canal bank a warmly familiar frantically barking dog hurled himself against her legs, practically knocking her down, and then she knew she was home. Bending to scratch Prince's head and let him lick her face, she was surprised that he went on barking aggressively at her companion even when she ordered him to stop. The man didn't appear to mind. He bade her a courteous goodnight at her gate, and left her sorry she hadn't asked his name or told him hers. She hoped she would some time see him again as she busied herself about getting Prince's long delayed supper. The dog's routine of welcome had a touch of reproach in it but as soon as he'd eaten he came in and put his paws on her shoulder to lick her face before jumping up on her bed where he always slept, a permanent foot-warmer in winter.

It was towards the end of January that she met her rescuer again, and at once recognised his friendly voice. He had a face to go with it, a reddish healthy face surrounded by curly greying dark hair. His smile showed good teeth and she liked the neatness of his polished shoes, his well-brushed napp overcoat, his rolled umbrella. He wasn't a tradesman; that was almost certain.

"I've often looked out for you," he smiled, attempting to stroke Prince who growled and (to her surprise) ran away, his tail straight as a brush.

"I caught a heavy cold over the Christmas and couldn't shake it off," Delia explained. "Prince had to take his own walks for a change."

"Too bad," he said. "And how are you feeling now?"

"Better thank you. And yourself?"

"Tough as an old boot," he said. "Haven't caught a cold since I stopped wearing a hat four years ago. That was after the mother died, God rest her."

"Oh, that's a strange coincidence." Delia felt free to chatter on at last and she told him about her mother who died four years ago too, and heard about this. They were both the last remnants of large families who had scattered out into the world, so this was another bond between them. He told her his name was Thomas Caffrey and he used to be an insurance collector. She thought it better not to let him know that the only job she'd ever had was sorting dirty clothes in a laundry, so she told him how she'd always had to take care of her mother which wasn't too far from the truth. The next day she met him he asked her was she ever in town and if so, could he give her tea one day in the Country Shop. That was a very respectable sort of suggestion as well as very kind, and she enjoyed the tea. He said he had his lunch there every day because they made beef-steak pies the very same as his mother's. She invited him to lunch in Albert Terrace, and when she went to visit the Cronins on Tuesday they wanted to hear all about it. Her friend Nora Cronin had doubts about Mr Caffrey. He seemed, she said, a fast worker, and Delia had to defend him.

"That first night he showed me where my own hall door was he didn't even tell me who he was or ask me who I might be. That was no fast worker," Delia said indignantly. "All I had to guide me was my own instinct and it told me he was a nice respectable man whose intentions I'd have no call to doubt."

"All the same . . . I'm not sure I like the sound of him," Nora Cronin said doubtfully.

"I don't know what you're talking about at all," Delia said again impatiently. "Would you like me to bring him over so that you can inspect him?"

"Why don't you do that?" her cousin said unexpectedly, and so Delia had a lot to occupy her mind for the next couple of weeks.

They had got to the Tom and Delia stage in the Country Shop and he had said he would see her soon again, he hoped. She had not liked to seem too eager. She had said she would be busy for the next week so would he leave it until the week after? He had no objection. He said he'd write her a postcard and then they could meet and decide where they might like to go. Perhaps take a tram to Howth some fine Sunday? Or would that be better left until Eastertime? Eastertime. Delia turned over the pleasant word in her mind and decided it was nice to be able to look that far ahead and know that in his mind the friendship would still be going strong. But all the same, it was a mistake to seem too eager in a case like this. She thought Nora Cronin with all her experience would be a useful guide to the rate of progress but all she had to say was be careful. That wasn't much help. But on the other hand her suggestion to bring him over was a good one. It would show him that she didn't lack friends. It would show him that some people other than himself took an interest in her, and it would show him the nice comfortable class of people she came from.

But getting around to asking him was another thing. Suppose he never did write that postcard? Well, if he didn't, she supposed she'd meet him one day walking the dog but in that case would it be in order for her to issue any sort of invitation at all? She tried to imagine what her mother would say, what advice she might be given, but all she could remember was the hostile reception any caller of hers had always received. Mary's friends and Nancy's and even Mollie's were not unwelcome and indeed were sometimes bidden to Sunday tea even before the various engagements took place. But Delia could never bring along a young man who had received her mother's approval. One by one (and there had only been three who ever showed the slightest interest) they had been frozen away from the house and she had been discouraged even from writing her excuses. Two she knew were long since married but she didn't know about the third, the nicest of them all, Domenic. Maybe it was time for her to make up her own mind. Maybe if she didn't get a postcard before the end of the week she should write her own postcard inviting him to Cronin's. He had given her his address and told her he would welcome a visit from her if ever she were walking his way. His landlady was very nice and they could have a chat and probably tea in the parlour. So in a way she had an open invitation, but she didn't tell Nora Cronin that. Fast worker wouldn't be strong enough criticism if she'd given away that much.

Anyhow her doubt was resolved before the end of the week when a very neatly written postcard came through her letter box. He had enjoyed her company so much last week that he would like to see her again if she wasn't too busy. Too busy! Delia had a good laugh over that, and she joked to Prince (who understood a joke as well as any Christian) when he trotted along beside her to post the letter. Her mother had always told her that to answer a postcard by a postcard (provided you didn't begin Dear X as in a letter) was quite sufficient but that if you wrote a letter you were showing respect as to an older person or somebody who had earned your gratitude. So a letter it had to be. A very carefully written letter on lined paper because she could never keep the slope at bay. Even with lined paper she had ended up throwing the finished letter into the fire and beginning all over again.

> Dear Tom,
> How are you keeping? It was nice to hear from you again and I look forward to seeing you soon.

Was that too forward altogether? If you made yourself cheap, she could hear the hectoring old voice say, you could hardly blame people for taking you at your own valuation. But it couldn't be making herself cheap, could it, when he had written first and said he would like to see her again if she wasn't too busy? After all, that was a very nice way of putting it, knowing her situation. So more confidently she continued, face bent to the strengthening light of a February morning . . . "I wonder would you like to accompany me next Tuesday when I visit my cousins for tea as usual over on the North side? Nora would be delighted to meet you . . ."

She stopped there, tore up the sheet of paper and began again. Saying Nora would be delighted to meet him was going a bit too far, and it suggested anyhow that there had been gossip and assumptions made. At last she was satisfied with the tone of the letter and after she had posted it she took Prince for a walk along the canal. There was always something about the lift of his tail to tell you that better weather and warm patches of sunshine were on the way. In the winter Prince hugged the fire like herself; when the year turned as she suddenly realised it had done now, he often spent hours out of doors by himself, snuffling along the canal banks and sometimes finding himself a lady friend. He was still only eight years old, and from her long experience of Princes she thought she could probably count on his company for at least five years more before bad sight, failing kidneys or lungs made life such a misery for him that she would have to think about Mr Lambert and the mercy of his injections. What sort of thought was that of a spring day bright with sunshine, with crocuses already opening in the warmth? Early crocuses were pale mauve and small with golden hearts. The later ones near Easter time were darker and bigger and made a more splendid show, but she liked the early ones best because they freely multiplied in the moist waterside soil and you could forget them every year until more than ever of them came up unasked the next time.

"Mine arc out too." Tom's voice said behind her, where she had stopped to admire a particularly fine patch of crocuses that had spilled out of one of the back gardens almost onto the banks of the canal. "You should come and see them!"

She was embarrassed as much by meeting him after writing as by the frenzied barking of Prince who started to snap at the turnups of his trousers and had to be smacked away. "It's too early to go home anyway, Delia, on such a nice afternoon."

She agreed and as they strolled among dogs and shouting boys and young women muffled up wheeling babies out in their go-cars she was surprised all over again at how naturally he could talk about this and that, even talk away her mumbled embarrassment over meeting him after she had posted a letter to him. Finally after a cup of tea from his landlady in the small overcrowded front room, Delia had relaxed enough when the woman went away to tell him even about the letter and the invitation it contained. He laughed and said getting the letter would be an added pleasure to look forward to but he must warn her in advance that he had every intention of accepting. So that was all right, better really than worrying over a reply. When they came out at last she admired the crocuses again in the front garden and was delighted when he admitted to planting them himself. The sun had vanished into a bank of smoky pinkish clouds and Prince was no longer barking outside the front gate. Sulking, no doubt, and gone on home by himself. Oh well, she'd had a pleasant afternoon anyhow and Tom walked her as far as her own gate and said, "Till Tuesday then," with a big smile.

"Tuesday," she smiled back at him, glad that it was only five days away. There was plenty to keep her busy in the garden meantime. There was an added reason for keeping it properly when somebody would notice: a man who planted crocuses in his landlady's front garden, no less! A man who would think of doing that had to be a good person. She was quite certain Nora would like him and Nora's husband Jack Cronin as well.

They didn't however, and Delia couldn't understand how the evening went so badly. She could see Tom had taken trouble over his appearance and he looked even more dapper than usual. A silver grey three-piece suit went with the grey hair and his dark grey napp overcoat was brushed and rich looking. If his heels were down a bit, the black shoes were polished to a glitter and his wine-coloured tie looked brand new. He paid her all the little attentions she sometimes wondered that other women took for granted, handing her first up on the tram, standing aside until she had her seat taken, paying the two fares. He joked about how long it was since he had been over the North side, remembering (as she did) childhood trips to Howth and Ireland's Eye, funerals he was taken to by cab in the Mariner's Church. At Fairview, where they got off the tram, he bought a box of chocolates for Nora in Edges, but it made no difference. Nora took the chocolates with the most perfunctory thanks and didn't open them. In fact she left them on the hallstand, so there was nothing to break the slight awkwardness of the introductions in the front room. Delia wished the children had been smaller, at the stage when their frocks or their new shoes could have been admired and you might be able to ask them to recite a poem they had learned in school. These tall fellows of fourteen and fifteen shook hands briefly and vanished about their own affairs. The girls stayed to talk for a while longer but they seemed ill at ease and soon went away too. When Nora went to see to the tea she was left with Jack who seemed to have taken an instant dislike to his guest.

"Where was this you said you worked?" he asked for surely the third time, and poor Tom had to tell him the Sun Insurance Company all over again.

"Then you must know an old butty of mine there by the name of Power!"

"There were several Powers," Tom said patiently.

"There were the Powers that be all right," Jack agreed heavily and laughed in a way that wasn't friendly. "Apart from them I never heard of any bar the one Andy Power that covered the Ringsend Irishtown area."

"He may have been a little after my time," said Tom still patiently.

"Tom has been retired for a few years now," Delia said. "He retired early to look after his mother."

"I see," Jack said, in a tone that suggested he didn't see at all, and then he had the rudeness to pick up the evening paper and turn to the Sports results.

"What won the 3.30?" Tom enquired pleasantly like a man who has decided to talk to a difficult acquaintance about what interests him.

"Weekend Cottage," said Jack shortly, and then relented a bit to add, "The last nag I backed is running yet."

"I had a small interest myself in Gypsy," Tom smiled. "I expect she's running yet too."

"As a matter of fact she fell on the second lap," Jack offered, just a shade friendlier and Delia thought the evening might be saved yet. But her optimism proved out of place. Over tea, Nora went on and on about people he should know if he lived in Harold's Cross where she had lived herself before marriage. Finally, one of the names evoked some response in Tom and Delia relaxed again. But after this it was even worse.

"You mean you must be the Tom Caffrey that went to Birmingham, that had the sister in the Poor Clares and the brother mixed up to his neck with all that embezzling trouble in the E.S.B.?"

"No, no." Tom wasn't smiling any more. Even Delia

could see the conversation had taken a turn he didn't like. "They were distantly related, that family, but it so happens that all my own brothers and sisters emigrated when they were very young. There was only Mother and myself after my father died. Your elder daughter is a remarkably fine looking girl, Mrs Cronin," he said when Joan excused herself and left the table.

"Handsome is as handsome does," Nora said sourly. "How about another cup of tea?"

"I will, it's delicious," Tom gallantly said and Delia remembered with amazement all the joking carefree evenings she had spent in this house and contrasted them with the anxiety in her throat now which threatened to choke her. She thought the evening would never end and going home on top of the tram she tried to find words of apology but ended up close to tears. Long before they reached Leonard's Corner, Tom's determinedly cheerful store of chat ran out and they were both silent.

"It seems I made a mess of it, Delia," he said at last, just before her own stop came. "I'm sorry."

"I could die of shame the way they treated you," Delia burst out at last, as they walked along to the canal bridge. "It wasn't your fault at all. You couldn't have been nicer. I can't believe they were so unfriendly."

"Perhaps they sensed I'm fond of you, Delia. Perhaps they had decided in their own minds you would never marry and they may even have had expectations. You own a nice little house after all?" There was a shade of enquiry in his voice.

"So do they," Delia said, rushing to defend her relations. "If that's what you think I'm sorry for you, because you don't know the Cronins at all." Indignation had made her overlook what he had just said, and when she realised it she blushed up to her ears, glad of the darkness to hide her confusion. "Perhaps they sensed I'm fond of you Delia." She didn't think she'd ever get the sound of that out of her head. Fond of her. She thought of asking him in for a cup of tea but it was too late and he might get the wrong idea.

Might get as wrong an idea of her as he had of the Cronins. A flurry of heels almost knocked her down only for his guiding arm linked in hers and then the shrill welcoming barks of Prince broke out.

"Attaboy," Tom said, bending down to stroke the animal, but instantly the barks of welcome changed to such savage growling that she said goodnight very quickly and almost ran in with the dog.

"I'll be in touch soon," Tom called after her. "Thank you for a very pleasant evening in *your* company at any rate." When she looked back he was gone in under the shadow of the bridge and for a moment she almost wanted to call him back. Instead she went indoors and busied herself about the dog's supper, blushing again when the ring of that sentence sounded in her ears. Perhaps they sensed I'm fond of you Delia. It was no use pretending to herself she wasn't fond of him too. She knew she would run like a young one every morning to the letterbox until she found another neatly written postcard.

When it came at last she thought the tone of it was a little less friendly than before the visit to the North side, but maybe she only imagined it. He wanted her to meet him at the Pillar and perhaps take a tram to the Zoo where they could have tea in the Gardens. She wrote back saying she'd love that and thanks for inviting her. The letter only had to be written once and she found to her surprise she wasn't nervous about writing to him any more. But when she met him on the Wednesday he looked so serious and she thought pale in the spring sunshine that she wondered aloud if he'd had a cold or even a touch of the 'flu. He said no, he was fine, and turned suddenly to buy her a bunch of violets from one of the women at the Pillar. He smiled when he saw the delighted fuss she made over a little thing like that and she thought of telling him that nobody had ever in her life given her flowers before. But her mother's loud voice telling her not to be a fool as usual came back to her with such violence that she stammered instead, and fumbled for a pin to fix the nosegay in her coat. Just after they stepped on to the 14 tram he remembered something and snapped his fingers. When they sat down inside he took a pin out of his coat lapel and stooped to fix the flowers for her. It was a good start to the afternoon.

By the lake in the Zoological Gardens he had another good idea. He left her for a moment and came back with a twopenny package of biscuits which they broke like children and fed to the ducks. The air was soft as milk and the whole Gardens seemed to be coming alive again after the long winter. She told him that the last time she'd fed the ducks here was with Nora's children when they were little ones. It only seemed like the other day, and look at them now. His face changed suddenly and she realised that once again she'd put her foot in it. Only a fool would spoil this lovely afternoon by reminding him of the other day.

The afternoon, however, was not spoiled. They strolled and chatted, past the fleshy flamingoes with their spiralling heads, around by the sea-lions' pool, already faintly misted with green where the willows trailed into the water. He said it seemed only last year he'd taken his mother here, and hired a wheelchair from the entrance and the old lady had insisted on waiting until the sea-lions were fed. She loved to see them diving for fish, and so clever about catching it when it was thrown to them on the rocks. As he talked they watched the sleek somnolent heads just beneath the oily surface of the pool; it was past their feeding time and there would be no gymnastics now. She asked him some more about his mother, feeling it might help if he talked about it. Once he got started he went on and on, mostly about the expenses of her last illness, which had eaten into his savings. In fact he had had to borrow money before the end and was still repaying it. Delia murmured her sympathy and wondered over the lovely afternoon tea he gave her in the Members' Restaurant, whether it would be crude to tell him that she had a little put by in the Building Society (apart from owning her own house), and she managed very well on the interest. If at any time he wanted to borrow a few pounds she'd be only too delighted . . .

She was never afterwards too sure how she found the words or the courage to express her eagerness to help. What was certain was that he didn't mind. Across the starched white tablecloth he took her hand in both of his and she thought she had never seen such honesty as shone out from his eyes under the curly grey hair.

"You're too tender-hearted for your own good Delia my dear. I wouldn't dream of taking advantage of you. I've always managed somehow and if one works steadily away at paying off even the largest debt it will eventually be wiped out. Believe me, I'm not worried and I don't want you to be."

"But it's the business of friends to help one another," Delia protested. "And I'd only be too delighted Tom . . ."

"My dear girl, don't say another word. Let's order some more of these tea-cakes – I can never resist them freshly baked, nor could Mother."

The elderly waitress took the order with a smile and a glance at the violets on Delia's coat. And Delia, who seemed to have spent her life smiling at the happiness of other people, blushed to think that another woman could smile like that at her.

Memory and Desire

THE television people seemed to like him and that was a new feeling he found exciting. Outside his own work circle he was not liked, on the whole, although he had a couple of lifelong friends he no longer cared for very much. The sort of people he would have wished to be accepted by found him arrogant, unfriendly, and not plain enough to be encouraged as an oddity. His wealth made him attractive only to the types he most despised. He was physically gross and clumsy with none of the social graces except laughter. Sometimes his jokes were good and communicable. More often they were obscure and left him laughing alone as though he were the last remaining inhabitant of an island.

Sometimes, indeed, he wondered if he spoke the same language as most other people, so frequently were they baffled if not positively repelled. He liked people generally, especially physically beautiful people who seemed to him magical as old gods. Sometimes he just looked at such people, not listening or pretending to listen to what they said, and then he saw the familiar expression of dislike and exclusion passing across their faces and he knew he had blundered again. Now for several weeks he had been among a closely knit group who actually seemed to find his company agreeable. He knew nothing about television and seldom watched it. But because his father's small glassmaking business had blossomed under his hand and become an important element in the export market, the television people thought a programme could be made out of his success story, a then-and-now sort of approach which seemed to him banal in the extreme. He had given his eventual consent because time so often hung on his hands now that expansion had progressed as far as was practicable and delegation had left him with little to do except see his more lucrative contacts in Europe and the United States a couple of times a year.

The only work he would actually have enjoyed during these days was supervising the first efforts of young glass-blowers. Two of the present half-dozen were grandsons of his father's original men. At a time when traditional crafts were dying out everywhere or falling into strange (and probably passing) hands, this pleased him. He tried to show signs of his approval while keeping the necessary distance right from the boys' first day at work, but this was probably one of the few places left in Ireland where country boys were shy and backward still, and their embarrassment had been so obvious that nowadays he confined himself to reports on them from the foreman. It had been different in his father's time. The single cutter and the couple of blowers had become personal friends of his father and mother, living in the loft above the workshop (kept warm in winter by the kiln) and eating with the family in the manner of medieval apprentice craftsmen. During holidays from boarding school, they had become his friends too, gradually and naturally passing on their skills to him, and so listening without resentment to the new ideas on design he had in due course brought back with him from art school and from working spells in Sweden. Gradually over the years of expansion after his father's death he had grown away from the men. Now since the new factory had been built in Cork he knew very few of them any more.

The odd thing about the television people was that right from the beginning they had been unawed and called him Bernard, accepting that he had things to learn about their business and that he would stay with them in the same guest-house, drink and live with them during the shooting of the film, almost as though they were his family and he an ordinary member of theirs. It had irritated and amused and baffled and pleased him in rapid progression and now he even found it hard to remember what his life had been like before them or how his days had been filled in. Their youth too had shocked him in the beginning; they seemed like children at play with dangerous and expensive toys. The director in particular (who was also the producer and therefore responsible for the whole idea) had in addition to a good-humoured boy's face an almost fatherly air of concern for his odd and not always biddable family. What was more remarkable, he could discipline them. The assistant cameraman who had got drunk and couldn't be wakened on the third day of the shooting had not done it again. When Eithne, the production assistant, had come down to breakfast one morning with a streaming cold and a raised temperature, Martin had stuffed a handful of her notes into the pocket of his jeans and sent her back up to bed, weeping and protesting that she was perfectly all right and not even her mother would dare to treat her like that.

Martin was very good with uncooperative fishermen, and with the farmer on whose land the original workshop still hung over the sea. A nearby hilly field had recently been sown with oats, and the farmer began with the strongest objection to a jeep laden with gear coming anywhere near it. He had agreed to it during preliminary negotiations, but shooting had in fact been delayed (delayed until more money became available) and that field, the farmer said, was in a delicate condition now. If they'd only come at the right time – Martin it was who finally talked him around with a guarantee against loss which would probably land him in trouble back in Dublin. But Martin (the Marvellous Boy was Bernard's private label for him) would worry about that one when he came to it and he advised Bernard to do the same about his fear of appearing ridiculous in some sequences. Not even half the stuff they were shooting would eventually be used, Martin said, and anyhow he'd give Bernard a preview at the earliest possible moment. Bernard stopped worrying again. Most of the time he had the intoxicating illusion of drifting with a strong tide in the company of excellent seamen and a captain who seemed to know his business.

The actual process of remembering was actually painful, of course. His only brother Tom had been swept away by a spring tide while fishing down on the rocks one day after school, and at first Bernard hadn't believed any reference to it would be possible when the script finally came to be written. Martin had come back to it casually again and again however, and finally one day of sharp March winds and flying patches of blue sky he had stood with Bernard on the headland near the roofless house.

"Let me show you what I have in mind," Martin said gently, the south Kerry accent soft as butter. "It will be very impressionistic, what I've in mind, a mere flash. A spin of sky and running tides, a moment. If you'd prefer, it won't need anything specific in the script. Just a reference to this friendly big brother mad about fishing, who knew about sea birds and seals and liked to be out by himself for hours on end. Maybe then, a single sentence about the nature of spring tides. The viewers generally won't know that spring tides have nothing to do with spring. You may say we're telling them about a successful glass industry, not about the sea, but the sea takes up a large part of your own early background and this piece is about you too. I'd write you a single sentence myself for your approval if you wouldn't mind – just to show you what I think would work – O.K.?"

" 'These are pearls that were his eyes' – you could end like that, couldn't you?" Bernard heard himself sneering and almost at once regretted it. The director actually blushed and changed the subject. In a few seconds it was as if the moment had never happened, but it seemed to Bernard that a kind of bond had been perversely established.

Two days later a spring tide was running and he watched a few sequences being shot that might well be used for the passage he knew now he was going to write. He walked away from the crew when he found he could no longer watch the sort of sling from which the chief cameraman had been suspended above the cliffs to get some of the necessary angles. The whole thing could have been done better and more safely by helicopter but Martin had explained about the problems he had encountered after overrunning the budget for the last production. It wasn't of course that he wanted to make Bernard's backward look a cheaper affair; you often got a better end result (in his own experience) by using more ingenuity and less money: he thought he knew exactly how to do it. The somewhat unconvincing argument amused and didn't displease Bernard, who thought it more than likely that something less conventional might finally emerge. The last he saw of the crew was that crazy young man, clad as always when working in a cotton plaid shirt, suspending himself without benefit of the cameraman's sling to try to see exactly what the lens saw.

A fit of nervousness that had in it something of the paternal and something else not paternal at all made him walk the seven miles around to the next headland. He hadn't thought like a father for five years. For half of that isolated time he hadn't brought home casual male encounters either because nothing stable had ever emerged from them and more often than not he was put off by the jungle whiff of the predator and managed to change direction just in time. Now he tried to resist looking back at the pair of boys busy with their games which they apparently regarded as serious. The head cameraman was even younger than Martin. He had a fair freckled face and red hair so long that it would surely have been safer to tie it back in a girl's ponytail before swinging him out in that perilous contraption. Bernard turned his face again into the stiff wind and looked back at the receding insect wriggling above the foaming tide, man and technology welded together in the blasting sunlight. The weird shape drew back his eyes again and again until a rock they called the Billygoat's Missus cut it off and he was alone for (it seemed) the first time in several weeks.

For the first time as in a camera's framed eye he saw his own room at home. Tidy as a well-kept grave, it was full of spring light from the garden. There were daffodils on his desk. Spangles of light from the rocky pool outside danced on the Yeats canvas that took up most of one wall and struck sparks from the two early balloons which he treasured. Five poplars in a haze of young green marked the end of his garden. Beyond it, the sharp-breasted Great Sugarloaf and eventually the sea. The room had been tidy for five years now. No maddening litter of dropped magazines, no hairpins, no shoes kicked off and left where they fell: left for the woman next morning to carry to the appropriate place in the appropriate room because she was born to pick up the litter of other people's lives, paid for it as the only work she knew. One night in a fit of disgust he had kicked into the corner a black leather clog, left dead centre on the dark carpet awaiting the exact moment to catch his shin. Uncontrolled fits of violence he despised. Recovering quickly he had placed the shoes side by side outside the door as though this were an old-fashioned hotel with a dutiful boots in residence. She had come in laughing later on, both clogs held up incredulously in her hand, laughing and laughing, tossing them finally up in the air to fall where they might before she left the room. As perhaps she had done last night and would do again tomorrow. Wherever she was.

A rising wind drove before it into the harbour a flock of black clouds that had appeared from nowhere, and when drops of rain the size of old pennies began to lash down he sought refuge in the hotel which had been small and unpretentious in its comfort when he was a child. His father's clients had often stayed here. He had sometimes been sent on messages to them with his brother. Now the place had several stars from an international guide book and was famous both for its seafood and the prices that foreign gourmets were willing to pay for it.

He sat in the little bar full of old coastal maps and looked out at the sea; alone for the first time in two weeks he was no less content than in the casual company of the television people. Their young faces and their voices were still inside his head. As though on cue, Martin suddenly came through into the bar, also alone. The wind had made any more shooting too dangerous for today he said, and the girls had gone off to wash their hair. He had his fishing gear in the boot, but he doubted if he'd do much good today.

"Have lunch with me, then, and eat some fish instead," Bernard invited, and was amused to see a flash of pure pleasure light up the director's face. Beer and a sandwich usually kept them going until they all sat down together at the end of the day.

"This place has got so much above itself even since the last time I was down here that I expect to be asked my business as soon as I set foot inside the door," Martin grinned.

"They wouldn't do that in late March," Bernard assured him. "Neither the swallows nor the tourists have arrived yet, so I fancy even people in your state of sartorial decay would be encouraged."

Martin took an imaginary clothes brush out of the jeans pocket (too tight to hold anything larger than a tooth-brush) and began to remove stray hairs from that well-worn garment which had seaweedy stains in several places and looked slightly damp. The boy walked with a sort of spring, like a healthy cat, and there was no trace yet of the flab which his pint-drinking would eventually bring. He ate the bouillabaisse and the fresh baked salmon which followed with the relish of a child brought out from boarding school for the day and determined to take full advantage of it. He praised the Alsace wine which was apparently new to him and Bernard decided that one of the great remaining pleasures of money was never to have to worry about the cost of anything one suddenly wanted to do. Bernard listened abstractedly to a little house politics over the coffee and then at the end of the first cognac he spoke one unwary line about buying all those bandy little boss men for a next birthday present for Martin should he wish it. The sea-reflecting blue eyes opposite him nar-rowed coldly for a moment before they closed in a bellow of laughter and the moment passed, like the rain outside. The sea was too uneasy, however, in the whipping wind to yield anything, but Bernard remembered one good story about his dead brother on a long-ago trip to Kinsale. Martin made a note in biro on the back of the wrist which held his fishing rod and Bernard knew it would be transferred to the mounting heaps of papers back at the hotel. More and more in the course of the programme he was being his own production assistant.

Mr O'Connor had carried in a mountain of turf for the fire and Eithne rather liked to listen to the rattle of the rain outside by way of contrast. Her hair was dry by now but spread all over the hearthrug and she swung it back in a tickling blanket over the recumbent John D who was still struggling with *The Irish Times* crossword.

"Give that over and sit up," she said, fetching her eternal dice-throwing version of Scrabble which she had bought somewhere in Holland.

"I was just going to work out another angle for that last shot to put to Martin when he gets back."

"Martin is probably half way to France by now on an ebbing tide. We'll find his pathetic little bits and pieces in the morning."

"Stop that!" John D was superstitious as well as red-haired. He was nervous about things like that. "All right, I'll give you three games and that's it."

"Nice John D. Did you notice Bernard's face today when you were strung up over the cliff, by the way?"

"I had other things to worry about. Is 'cadenza' allowed?"

"It's not English but I suppose it's in the OED like everything else – it's virtually been taken over, after all."

"O.K. it's allowed." John D formed the word.

"But no *brio* or *allegro molto,*" Eithne warned.

"No *brio* or *allegro molto* – I haven't the makings of them anyhow. What sort of look did Bernard have on his unlovely mug?"

"A bit nervous for you, I think. I think that's why he walked away."

"Arrogant bastard a lot of the time." John D swept up the dice after totting his score. "Are capitalists human? You should put that theme to Martin some time."

"More a Neville sort of line, surely? But I think you're wrong. He's shy and he's only just stopped being uneasy with us."

"Just in time to say goodbye then," said John D with satisfaction. "There's hardly a week in it, if the weather lifts a bit."

"If," Eithne said, scooping a single good score. It was her game, her thing, but the others always won. "I think he's lonely, which only goes to show you money isn't everything."

"You can be miserable in much more comfort though. He looks to me like a bod who's had it off wherever he pleased with one sex or t'other, despite his ugly mug. He has the brazen confidence you only get from too much money."

"I think you're wrong and the death of his brother is still bothering him after all these years. It's something I just have a hunch about. And then of course his wife walked out on him a few years ago. Prime bitch they say she was too. He came home one night and found not as much as a hairclip left behind, and his baby gone too."

" 'Hunch' is not a permissible word all the same. Thirties slang," said John D with finality. "Why wouldn't she walk out on him when he's probably given to buggery?"

"It's much more permissible than 'Cadenza'. How about to hunch one's shoulders?"

"Go and ask Mr O'Connor if he has a dictionary then."

"You go. My hair isn't dry yet."

"Your hair is practically on fire, lady," John D said, settling himself comfortably on the hearthrug again. A car crunched in the sandy drive outside and Eithne gave a long sigh.

"Thank God. I couldn't have borne the smell of good

country roast beef much longer."

"There'll be frogs' eyes to follow."

"At worst there'll be stewed apples, at best apple pie. Doesn't your nose tell you anything except whether a pint's good or bad?"

In out of the rain and the early dusk, Bernard was touched all over again by the sight of two apparent children playing a game beside the fire. He came over very willingly to join them when Eithne called and Martin went upstairs to look over his notes before dinner. He would call Evelyn on his way down, he said.

Later they all went in the pouring rain to the pub and listened while a couple of local Carusos rendered songs like 'Two Sweethearts' – one with hair of shining gold, the other with hair of grey – or the endless emigrant laments favoured by local taste. Whiskey chasing several pints made John D a bit quarrelsome and he shouted for a song from Bernard just to embarrass him. To everybody's surprise, Bernard was not embarrassed. He stood up, supported only by two small Jamesons (the second of which he was still nursing) and gave the company a soft-voiced but not untuneful version of 'Carrigfergus' which was vociferously applauded by the locals and earned him delighted approval from the team. Eithne thought they ought maybe incorporate 'Carrigfergus' into the soundtrack, and John D wanted to know why they couldn't all move up to Carrigfergus and let Bernard do his party piece with his back against the castle walls. This suggestion was received with the contempt it deserved, but Bernard wasn't discomfited.

That happened only when they got back to the guesthouse and he heard Martin telling Mrs O'Connor that they would almost certainly be finished shooting by the end of the week and would hardly stay over the weekend. The sinking of the heart was like what came long ago with the necessity of facing back to school after the long summer holidays. He felt ashamed of his emotion and unsure how to conceal it, so he went up early to his room. Normally they would hang about for hours yet, reading the newspapers they hadn't had time for during the day, swapping stories, doing crossword puzzles, discussing the next day's work. Usually he didn't contribute much to the conversation; like a silent member of a big family he was simply there, part of what was going on, perfectly content to sit up as long as they did.

Now there was something symbolic about hearing the murmur of their voices from downstairs. The script had still to be written and there would be consultations in Dublin about it, hopefully with Martin, but (give or take a few days from now) the thing was over. Next week they would all be busy taking somebody else through his mental lumber-room. The little family would re-form itself around another fire, and it would have nothing to do with him. And soon it would be April, breeding lilacs out of the dead land, mixing memory and desire. Time perhaps to go away; he had promised himself a few weeks in April. On the other hand, why not stay on here?

He let down the small dormer window and looked out over the water. This house echoed, in almost exact detail, that other, roofless, house; the murmur of voices, even, was like his sisters' voices before they settled down for the night, all together in the big back bedroom. His own small room above the harbour used to be shared with his brother. The rain had stopped now and there was almost no sound from the sea and he wasn't surprised when Martin came to his door to say the weather forecast had been very good for the south-west and they might get in a full day's shooting tomorrow.

"Come in and have a nightcap," he invited, and Martin said he wouldn't stay long but happily didn't refuse the brandy when it was taken from the wardrobe.

"What will you do next?" Bernard asked, just for a moment unsure of how to begin.

"A bit of a break before I join Current Affairs for a short stint," the boy smiled. "Yours is the last programme in the present series. No more now until next season."

"You mean you're going to take a holiday?" He strove to make his voice sound casual, although he was suddenly aware of the beating of his heart.

"Unless something untoward crops up, yes."

"Why not join me in Greece, then, since that's where I'm heading next week or the week after? The place I have on Ios needs to be opened up after the winter and there's plenty of room I assure you. Also two local women waiting to cook and clean for us." Bernard saw the refusal before it came; it was only a question of how it would be framed, how lightly he would be let down.

"It's a tempting offer, and there's nothing I'd enjoy more, all things being equal. Never been further than Corfu as a matter of fact. But my wife has organised a resident babysitter for the two boys and we're off on a busman's holiday to Canada as soon as I'm free. Laura is Canadian you know. I met her when I was training in London with the B.B.C. When we get back, maybe you'd come over for supper with us some evening? Laura's an unpredictable cook, but you'll agree that doesn't matter too much when you meet her. Is it a deal?"

He drained the glass and got up off Bernard's bed with the same catspring which was noticeable also in the way he walked.

"It's a deal. Many thanks. And maybe you'll both join me some time in Greece?"

Martin made the appropriate noises and didn't go at once, but started talking about a painter called Richard Dadd who (somebody had told him) had probably given Yeats his Crazy Jane themes. He hadn't seen the paintings himself at the Tate but Bernard had, so this kept them going until the door closed behind him, and on his youth, and on the hollow promise of knowing him as one knew every line of one's own hand. There was a lot of the night left and, fortunately, a lot of the brandy too.

The weather behaved as the weathermen said it would and the rest of the shooting went without a hitch. During this couple of weeks the year had turned imperceptibly towards summer, primroses in the land-facing banks, sea-pinks along the cliffs and an air about the television people that Bernard had seen before and couldn't quite place. Only when he went with them for the final day's shooting did he pin it down; a fairground the day after the circus. The television gear was more easily moved, of course; no long hours were needed for the pull-out. But the feeling was the same. They didn't believe him when he said he was staying on and they seemed shocked, which amused him, when he determinedly heaped presents on them the morning they were going: his Leica for Eithne who (incredibly) had never owned a camera of her own, a sheepskin jacket for John D because his own was in flitters from the rocks, a silver brandy flask (circa 1840), a cigarette lighter and a gold biro scattered apparently at random among the rest. The vulgarity of the largesse amused Bernard himself because such behaviour was not usual and he didn't entirely understand his impulse. But he understood perfectly why he gave Martin his signed first edition of 'The Winding Stair', a volume which for a year or more had lived in the right-hand door-pocket of his car for no better reason than that he liked to have it there. He had bought it somewhere along the quays of Cork.

> "Fair and foul are near of kin
> And fair needs foul," I cried,
> "My friends are gone and that's a truth
> Nor grave nor bed denied
> Learned in bodily loneliness,
> And in the heart's pride."

A former owner had marked that with a small star in the margin, and Martin smiled slightly as he read it aloud in gratitude when the book fell open.

"I often have a disturbing feeling when I finish a job like this that I know –" he searched patiently for the words he wanted and his hesitation seemed to Bernard like comfort consciously given for some loss he could understand. "That I know almost enough to begin over all over again.

Properly." He didn't smile at all when they shook hands so that the handgrip seemed warmer. "Until soon, in Dublin," were his last words, a rather childish farewell which would have left a pleasant glow behind if Bernard had not known by now that they would not meet again. The vanful of technology went on ahead of the boy's unreliable little red sports car, and watching from the drive of the guesthouse, Bernard had the feeling of the fairground again after the circus caravans have rolled away. It was peaceful, though, with the blue sea breathing quietly all around him and a few mares' tails of cloud slowly unravelling in the sky.

He was leaning over the wall considering how he would fill his remaining time when the guesthouse owner strolled by, indicating the blue boat which bobbed at the end of its mooring rope below them. "You could take the aul' boat out fishing any day you had a fancy for it, Mr Golden. You're more than welcome to her any time though I wouldn't recommend today, mind you."

"I'm much obliged to you, Stephen. I have all the gear I need in the boot of the car so I might do just that. But why not today?"

"She'll rise again from the south-west long before evening," his host said positively. "And she'll below herself out if I'm not mistaken. 'Twould be a dangerous thing to go fishing out there today."

"The weather men last night didn't mention any gales blowing up."

"The weather men don't live around this Hook either," O'Connor said drily. "I've caught those same gentlemen out once or twice, and will again with the help of God."

"You might be right at that, I suppose. But if I do go out, I'll only fish for a short while, I promise you."

A pleasant man, Stephen O'Connor, a retired Civic Guard with an efficient wife to make a business out of the beautiful location of their house and her own hard work. Bernard remembered him vaguely from childhood, pedalling wet and fine around the coast roads, stopping here and there for a chat, missing nothing. It was he who had brought the news that Tom's body had been washed ashore somewhere near Kinsale. It was he who had in fact identified it. On remembering this Bernard toyed with the idea of having an actual conversation with this kindly man whose memories touched his own at one black juncture. The moment passed, however, and Stephen made a little more chat, lingering with natural courtesy just long enough for a guest to make up his mind whether or not further company would be welcome, and then he ambled contentedly in the direction of the greenhouse for a day's pottering. Old man, old man, if you never looked down again at a drowned face of my father's house it would be time enough for you. Forgive me, Stephen O'Connor.

The first warm sun of the year touched Bernard's eyes and he smiled, sitting up on the sea wall. No more Aprils, no more lilacs breeding out of the dead land, no more carnal awakenings. He felt peaceful, then a little surprised that the image behind his closed eyelids was not of his brother or of the young Martin or even of the caravans pulling out. It was the small wilful face of his daughter in the act of breaking away when one tried to hold her. He didn't know where she was, or even how she looked now, whether she still mirrored her mother in every gesture. He had a perfect right to know for the mere trouble of enforcing it. He hadn't done that, at first put off by the refusal of maintenance, by the eternal sound of the phone ringing in an empty flat and by two or three unanswered letters. He hadn't made a very energetic effort to keep in touch. As one year became two or three and now five, it had always seemed too late, but it would be untrue to pretend he greatly cared. It was just that, not being able to understand why the child's face should be so vivid in his mind, he was bothered as by some minor irritation, a door that slammed somewhere out of sight, a dripping tap. It wasn't until he was actually aboard the boat starting up the engine in a freshening breeze that he realised why he couldn't rid himself of his daughter's face today, of all days.

The Open House

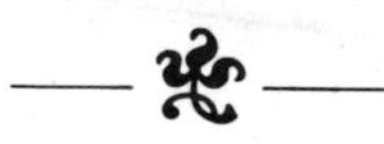

ONCE again the bell went jangling unanswered through the house. Once again Teresa wandered down the steps, and looked through into the book-walled room. This time, glasses stood about here and there, there were books on the floor, and several large bright pottery ashtrays, loaded with cigarette ends. It was a long room, and Teresa pushed her face against the glass to see through the back window and out into the garden. All she could see were the long waxen buds of a magnolia tree and a stretch of lawn and beyond that a greenhouse with (she was almost certain) a figure bent down inside it. She ran around to the other side of the steps, past another bay window with drawn curtains, and on to a small yellow door which *might* lead through to the back garden. Half fearfully, she pushed it open, amazed that it was not locked. She followed a little stony path through the massed crocus beds and tiny dwarf fir trees to the greenhouse. A dumpy elderly woman straightened up angrily and came out with her arms full of forced pink sticks of rhubarb.

"Well?" she said to Teresa, small eyes unfriendly in a pudgy pale face.

"Well, I couldn't get an answer, you see, and I came about the house."

"You can't see anybody about the house now – such a time to knock people up." Her small inquisitive eyes passed over the thin pink tweed coat and down to the white stockings which Teresa suddenly felt must be laddered, "and what would you be wanting to know about the house?"

Teresa lost her temper. "It *is* advertised for sale, you know. The address is given. And I came here yesterday afternoon and there was nobody in then either."

"So it was you yesterday, too?" the old face giggled. "Knocking fit to raise the dead." Teresa remembered the glasses in the convivial front room and felt very certain that this was a servant, not the owner, despite her air of assurance.

"Can you tell me when I could find the owner at home?"

"There's at home and at home in it," mumbled the old woman. "Ask me, and I'll tell you they're mad sorry already they put the place up for sale at all. All this will blow over, if you ask me."

"I can see it's no *use* asking you anything," said Teresa, and marched off in good order with her head high.

That evening after supper she persuaded Tom out with her. His interest in acquiring a house and crippling overheads was minimal, and he felt in fact quite satisfied with the cosy poky flat they rented for forty pounds a week. But Teresa's four sisters each had a bright box in the suburbs of Dublin and she dreamed of dazzling them with something different. To Tom she kept making references to the future family and the necessity of providing a room for every boy and girl. When he looked at her satirically over well-polished glasses, as he did now, she frequently burst into tears; but he never paid any attention so it never lasted long.

That evening, eventually, they gained entry. The door was opened by a tall abstracted-looking man in a knitted cardigan, who escorted them from room to room as though he were standing in for somebody else.

"Nice little box, this," he said, indicating what was clearly a maid's room at ground level. "Guaranteed to keep the working classes where they belonged – far away from the family. A girl could easily freeze to death down here with the minimum of inconvenience to everybody else. No fireplace, you see. No room for a wardrobe – she wouldn't have owned much apart from aprons anyway. They went in here."

He pulled open a small wall cupboard, and pointed to the suitcases lying about. "Matter of fact, we've used it as a boxroom since the last girl went. That was about thirty years ago; in my father's day. Our present housekeeper, who dates from just after the girl's time, has occupied for years the best bedroom in the house."

He had a high pedantic voice and warm friendly blue eyes. His forehead was high and his head pearshaped, dotted here and there with fuzz like that on an Easter chicken. He led them, vaguely making sounds of approval, from this to the breakfast room which had another queer oil painting above the fireplace, and on to the kitchen, so dazzling, so modern, so warm (despite the unfriendly presence of the greenhouse woman) that Teresa was rendered speechless by her desire to own it.

Tom had closed up completely and allowed himself to be steered along slightly worn but magnificent carpets up the curved staircase to the drawing-room. Teresa plucked him to notice the Waterford chandeliers, the velvet curtains, the auctioneers' showpieces on all sides. He grunted. He grunted again over the sunken pink bath and the black tiles, over the Georgian cheval glass in the second largest bedroom, and the nudes in heavy gilt frames.

"Don't fancy the Rubens type myself," their guide was saying. "All breasts and buttocks. Now look at this Manet. Different kettle of fish entirely, don't you see. Voluptuous but bony. By which I mean one is *aware* of the bones."

Tom examined the young girl in the painting and thought she looked no better than she should but (as the man said) considerably better than the buxom bathing beauties. He didn't know what to make of the black cat at her bare heels, so he laughed, the first sign of life from him since they entered the house.

Coming out of the room he hissed to Teresa, "Put this house out your mind, my lady. You'd buy the Mansion House for less."

Downstairs, in the book-walled room that had first attracted Teresa, they were surprised to find a crowd. There had been no sounds of a party in progress, and it was clear why. If this was a party it was the oddest one she had ever seen.

Young men lay about on the carpet, now and again lifting a book off the shelves and holding a consultation about it. A girl in jeans was clipping her toenails in front of the log fire, and a husband and wife (of course?) conducted a fierce though largely silent battle over near the stacked paintings.

All had drinks in various stages of consumption and all looked as comfortably unconcerned as though they lived here.

"Let me introduce you to Colin Healy," said their guide carelessly, and afterwards went to fetch them a drink. Teresa controlled herself with some difficulty and poked Tom surreptitiously.

"Hello," said Colin Healy, getting up politely off the carpet and bowing to Teresa. To her disappointment, he excused himself almost immediately and disappeared through the door. Teresa poked Tom again. "Did you hear who he is?" she whispered. "I know it's the same because I've seen his pictures heaps of times."

"What about it?" Tom muttered. "Let's get out of here now."

"We have to wait for the drinks. He's gone to get them."

Tom shrugged and sat down with assumed ease on a sheepskin. Nobody paid any attention to them, except the girl in front of the fire, who said to Teresa, "Do you happen to have any proper nail clippers in your bag?"

"Sorry," Teresa smiled, "Haven't I seen you somewhere before?" She knelt down beside the girl for a closer look.

"It's more than possible," the girl said. "Excuse me." Just as she was, in bare feet, she moved away to one of the young men, and Teresa sighed. Now she knew where she'd seen the girl before – on the gossip page of an evening newspaper at the opening of an art exhibition two nights before. At the opening of her *own* exhibition.

Soon the abstracted blue-eyed man came back with their drinks, and Tom cleared his throat. "Perhaps you could tell us approximately what you expect for the house?" he said, and Teresa thought, how rude – couldn't he have waited until later?

"We must have a long talk about that, old chap – it's a rather difficult situation. Come back tomorrow evening and have a bite with us – then we'll see." Somewhere at one end of the room someone had started to strum a guitar and their host moved in its direction, taking Teresa by the hand with him. "Come and meet Matt Taylor."

Before a week was out, Teresa's diary had been scribbled all over on the back of the cover with famous names. Every night when they returned home to their empty flat she wrote down – lest she forget to tell her sisters – the names of new celebrities, or anyhow names she had forgotten to note on previous evenings.

Mostly there was a solid core of the same people, and with these she became fairly familiar. So she informed Tom, who sometimes demurred at yet another evening at the Wilkinsons, but usually accompanied her with a sort of resigned but growing pleasure.

All they had learned about the house was that if they produced cash (which with the help of Teresa's money and an agreed bank loan, they could), the price would be tempting and most of the carpets would be thrown in. Some of the other furnishings they could buy reasonably if they wished – the things that wouldn't travel well.

It was Tom who finally found out the reason for the sale. Mr Wilkinson – whom Teresa had long since begun to call Roger – was in danger of being closed on by his bank for a larger (horrifyingly large, it seemed to Tom) sum of money. This had been guaranteed two years ago for a poet who was emigrating with his wife and six children to the United States. The poet had paid the interest for a while, but had now stopped. Somewhere on that sizeable continent, he had simply disappeared.

"Couldn't you just pay the interest?" Tom had enquired.

"I could, but that's a life sentence. I prefer to pull out while the going's good."

"Doesn't bother you at all – I mean, morally?"

"Not at all. You must consider, after all, that *I* didn't borrow the money. And Monaghan's talents are such that in a rational society, like Florence during the Renaissance or medieval Ireland, for instance, he would have been supported either by the state or by a rich patron. My bank now has the honour to be a rich patron of the arts – why should the whole matter cost me one wink of sleep? This house is practically all I have, old chap, and Jennifer has nothing but an occasional sale at an occasional show and her exceptionally beautiful eyes."

Jennifer, it appeared, was the girl in jeans (only half his age) whom they had seen attending to her toenails. She seldom spoke to them but they had grown not to mind.

Occasionally Tom wondered if he was helping with a criminal transaction, but his office colleagues assured him he mustn't be a fool. He was getting the house for about three-quarters of the current market value, and the value of such houses was going up and up every year. It was an investment, his colleagues kept telling him, and he began to feel more confident about it.

One evening when Teresa was fully occupied with a school of young painters in the corner, Wilkinson beckoned Tom to come out of the room with him.

Conspiratorially he led the way to the small study in the front of the house and closed the door. Tom sank into a glorious old-fashioned leather smoking chair and looked apprehensively at his host, who offered him a cigar. Over the business of lighting this, he said in a clearly worried tone, "I'm afraid a snag has cropped up, old chap."

"Yes?" Tom said, even more worried.

"It's Mary-Ann, you see. Been with the family for forty years – best years of her life and so forth. She's nearly seventy now and unemployable, I should think, though she's as good a worker as ever. The plan was of course to take her with us to London, but it won't work."

"Why?" Tom said.

"Because, quite simply, she won't come. Some peasant

fear of what she calls a pagan country or something. Or just plain unwillingness to undertake the bother of moving. At any rate her mind is entirely made up so there's only one thing to do. We'll have to let her go to you with the house, old chap. If you agree you can have her and the carpets and the things Teresa has taken a fancy to for the fifty thousand. Now I can't be fairer than that."

"But," Tom suddenly shouted, "we haven't bought or sold slaves on this island since the time of St Patrick!"

Wilkinson's face looked pained. "Of course you would still pay her, old fellow. Just as we do."

"How much?" asked Tom faintly.

"Ten pounds a week and two half-days and every second Sunday off."

And so it was settled. Teresa, much to his relief, seemed to regard the arrangement as perfectly natural, although he remembered how she had frequently expressed dislike of the old woman. But Teresa was hardly herself these days. She had abandoned her white lace stockings for jeans and shaggy sweaters and she seldom came in without several newly-purchased secondhand books stuffed into the shopping bag.

On the night the Wilkinsons left, Tom and Teresa went to the North Wall to see them off, in company with many of the faithful. They weren't flying because, although so much of the heavier stuff had been sent on in a sealed truck, a great deal of baggage remained, too much for flying.

They trooped aboard, dumped the baggage and stormed into the bar. Jennifer was crying and so was Teresa but most of the company were in good spirits, and arrangements for meetings in London were bandied about. When the final hooter shrilled out, there was much embracing of everybody by everybody else. Wilkinson gripped Tom's hand in a fraternal farewell.

Outside on the quay in the drizzling cold of a spring night, Teresa and Tom suddenly found themselves alone. "Never mind," said Teresa brightly, "they'll probably be at home before us." He opened the car door and she jumped in, and in the small light of the dashboard Tom carefully examined her face.

"Who will?" he said.

"Well, who do you think?" she shrugged impatiently. "Everybody."

It was now Tom's turn to shrug but she didn't notice. He drove fast through the web of fine rain that had cocooned the city, and when they got back to the house it was in darkness, with only one light burning upstairs in the old woman's room.

Teresa made exasperated noises and raced two at a time up the granite steps to the door. As soon as she let herself in she switched on the two carriage lamps on either side of the door, and then ran downstairs, leaving the door open for Tom. Downstairs she stood still for a moment and listened to the house.

It was quiet, except for Tom's footsteps, and it didn't feel so much like itself as like the hated flat they would never see again. True, the grandfather clock ticked away in the lower hall – it had been a present to her from Roger – but there was something wrong. Teresa sniffed like a dog in a strange place and pushed open the living-room door, her favourite room in all this lovely house.

Darkness. No fire. And the stars of rain glinting on the dark windowpanes. What *had* Mary-Ann been about? Why hadn't she lit the fire as usual at five o'clock? True, with the central heating, it wasn't *strictly* necessary, but conviviality was hardly possible without the friendly focus of a fire. And it always *had* been lit. The room didn't look too bare because of the carpet, but of course it would be better when their own furniture arrived tomorrow.

She wandered down the three steps to the kitchen and it too was in darkness. She stretched out her arms to its warm functional beauty and brushed a finger against a note left under a teapot on the solid oak counter. She read: "I thought 'twould be foolish lighting the fire across in the room with only your two selves in it. There's a beef stew and an apple cake I made for ye in the slow oven. Mary-Ann."

When Tom came in, rather superior and proud and very pleased with himself, Teresa showed him the note angrily. "She's right," Tom said, putting on the kettle for coffee. "What would we want with a fire when the heating is switched on since morning? It won't be any time before we notice the saving on coal. And how did the old girl know I go for hot apple cake?"

"But you can't properly entertain without a fire – you know that."

"Never mind about that. We're not entertaining, not this evening whatever. I was going to ask the brother over but I thought better of it. Too tired after all the pullyhauling around of the last few days. God, I *am* tired!" He threw himself down on a windsor chair and stretched and yawned.

"Well *I'm* not tired – the idea!" Teresa angrily asserted. "You'd never know who might be here any minute."

"I would know," said Tom, with the knowing grin she had never liked. "Sweet damn nobody, that's who, and that's the way I like it. The amount of crap I've listened to in the last few weeks!"

"Very well," said Teresa, angry again. "You do exactly what you like. I shall be at home tonight and any other night to anyone who drops in. If not tonight, then certainly tomorrow – don't you remember what a night Saturday always was in this house?"

"Look, Teresa –" Tom began kindly, but just then the door-bell sounded loudly.

"*Now*, Tom Dunne," Teresa said triumphantly and ran away to the door. She came back with bent head, scuffling marks on the tiles with the tips of her rubber-soled shoes.

"It was our next-door neighbour. Wants to know if we have everything we need."

"Very civil," Tom said. "Have some coffee."

"I don't want any, thanks. I think I'll wait."

"Come on, Teresa. First cup in our own kitchen in our own house?"

"Well . . ." Smiling doubtfully, she sat down beside him and accepted the cup. "Tomorrow we'll light the fire early and get in some beer. Saturday is the biggest night of the week, remember."

"Certainly," Tom said, "certainly." Teresa, placated, smiled at him above the rim of her coffee cup.

She had a warm vision of cheerful society, of herself casual in a paint-stained smock. Tom was cheerful also, stretching out stockinged feet to the kitchen range, thinking that he liked the house after all. Much cosier than the flat. And just as quiet.

A Friend of Don Juan

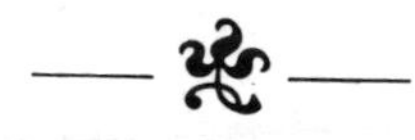

THE straps cut sharply into his collarbones and a part of the steel frame lay unkindly against his vertebrae. Heavy mist which had blown in over Bray Head beaded his eyebrows and when he bent to the slope, water stung his eyes. Far ahead, on the long straight before you got onto the shoulder of the mountain, Dermot and Rachel played careless as children, in a gap of sunshine from which the mist had peeled away. William stopped for a moment to watch them, and they waved to him before striding on arm in arm, jerseys removed and knotted around their waists. He might as well be a porter for all the attention they paid to him, but then he should be used to that. In all the years since he and Dermot had come down from college together, the girls were changing constantly, but never the situation.

Bracing himself, he took the remaining hilly tussocks between him and the straight bed of a little stream, ignoring the pressure of the rucksack and his stinging watery eyes. If that skinny Rachel could carry it from home to the bus-stop, he could get it to the top of this mountain without too much bother. Coming down, it would certainly be lighter. It might even be carried by Dermot, who frequently offered help when the need for it had practically vanished. This however was unlikely. He would be fooling around with Rachel on the way down, in playful mood probably, with her hair perhaps opened out of its long plait and wrapped around his own neck, and he would be singing at the top of his voice.

Dermot might play at independence but he could never get far without him in most circumstances. The man would frequently come out penniless, with only a cheque book as a proof to the world that he was not really without money. William never saw him short. Even when he made promises to two women for the same evening, William could be relied on to sort out the situation. Just as, at the end of every affair, William could be relied on for help towards a smooth exit.

Sometimes he couldn't remember clearly the faces of the girls who had wept out their loss of Dermot into his tweed jacket, but he could remember their names. Even in college there had been Mary and Sarah and Fidelma and Hilary and Joan; and Eithne, of course, the wife of a very junior lecturer. By way of breathing space after that brief but extremely scandalous affair (for which in justice Dermot could not be held wholly responsible), William had advanced the air fare to Germany, where money for a Greek holiday could be earned by factory work. In Greece he had offered Dermot the benefit of his somewhat unoriginal but useful advice. From the time of Helen of Troy onwards, no good had come to any man from helping himself to a slice of cut cake. All right, so wives had had their problems and they were sometimes available and seldom disappointing. But they were always more trouble than they were worth, and breaking with them was twenty times more emotionally charged than breaking with a girl. To everything Dermot said yes, of course William was right, and until the advent of the American girl, Mary Louise in Crete, he had been the best and most rational of companions. During the Mary Louise episode he had been considerably less trouble than in similar circumstances at home, and when he passed on to an English art student named Jennifer from Croyden, Mary Louise had been unusually generous to William.

In fact his ears still burned whenever he remembered that she had said his face was straight out of Rembrandt, not beautiful exactly but warm and reassuring. She said she *liked* prominent teeth that no American dentist had ever been allowed to reduce to the conformity of everybody else's, and no, a large nose the shape of his did not worry her too much. All this by way of a prelude to proving it couldn't possibly have worried her at all. William smiled at the astonishing memory, and set off briskly in the direction of his friends.

Rachel was sitting on Dermot's rolled-up jersey and he had one of her boots off, her bare foot resting between his knees. William smiled, remembering she had held out longer than anybody else against him – fully three months now.

"What's wrong?"

"Nothing that a plaster won't fix," Dermot said, businesslike. "You've got one, haven't you?"

Of course he had. He bent to examine the blister, which had already broken, and then he made his selection from several plasters in his pocket. Rachel winced when he touched her foot. Stray wisps of blonde hair had escaped her thick plait and curled childishly around her face, beads of mist clinging to them.

"I won't hurt you," William assured her, "hold on." Dermot held the foot in the right position until the sticking plaster with its soothing lint was in place. Rachel sighed.

"Sweet William," she said, smiling at him. She had babyish teeth and a downy freckled face. Her bones were light as a bird's and he hardly noticed her weight when she allowed him to pull her up by one hand. Dermot, his eyes straining towards the sea, hushed them suddenly. "Listen," he said.

They listened in the warm damp air but heard nothing except the wind in the heather that sounded like the distant wash of the tide. Suddenly Dermot mimicked a cuckoo's call, liquid and accurate, and again he motioned them to silence. Then they heard it coming from the woods outside the village.

"Cuck---oo."

"Summer is icumen in," Rachel sighed happily. "First time I've heard the cuckoo for three years. He belongs to school holidays."

"Neither of you heard him the first time?" Dermot asked a little contemptuously. Neither of them had, and he looked smug before hooking his arm through Rachel's and attempting to walk her off.

"Wait," Rachel said, "I've got apples." The mist was by now unmistakably thinning around them, and yellow spills of sun dazzled back at them from the distant sea. They sat down on a rock.

Rachel took off her blue cotton shirt and, still munching, lifted up her closed eyes to the sun. Underneath she was wearing a tee-shirt of the same blue, cut away from thin freckled shoulders. Dermot removed his shirt too, and William felt his own cling to the prickly skin under the rucksack, under the tweed jacket. Even if he were not the official carrier he wouldn't shed his clothes anyway, however hot the day might become, because he had never learned to do things like that naturally.

He smiled however as he pulled back again into the slope. Without Dermot he wouldn't even have heard that bird, or earned that Sweet William from Rachel. Once he had tried climbing Djouce alone and for a while had savoured his freedom from tackle. In his pocket were only some fruit, some chocolate, and a change of socks. His mother had warned him he had to be careful with feet like his, if he ever aimed to court a girl. It had been a warm July day, with tender hazy sunlight and a small breeze. He hadn't enjoyed it.

But today the countryside opened and bloomed about him. The bitter almond smell of the gorse stung his nostrils. Was it Dean Swift who had said it smelled like the marriage bed? A skylark spun crazily above his head, the spiral of its song winding back down to him. He remembered Djouce again, when the day had been more beautiful, but it hadn't been the same. He had been free and it had been flavourless, nothing to involve his attention or to spur him into disapproval. He didn't really approve of Dermot's activities and especially of the present game with Rachel, whose parents had no doubt taken care for all of her nineteen years that she would meet none but nice Jewish boys with honourable intentions.

Until she went to college, that is. Until in her second year as a law student a celebrated former chairman of her debating society – Dermot – had been invited back to take over a rather important public discussion. William had attended, and he had seen the opening gambit of the familiar game. Absolute attention to every word that Rachel said. An adroit piece of public gallantry which Rachel had not rejected. The careful invitation to supper afterwards with *both* of them. How could the girl have known? William had even detected her slight surprise at his presence, but that was familiar ritual too, if only she had known it.

There were times when William felt he must know how God felt, having seen everything before. It was possible to intervene, but the rules forbade it. You watched. You assisted if asked. You waited. You offered consolation or understanding at the end, and these were your functions. You didn't overstep them. Once William's own elderly father had said to him in bafflement, "What sort of fellow fritters his life away playing gooseberry for a pup that will find himself a lonely old man at the end of all his andrew-martins? Let you go out and find *yourself* a nice girl before it's too late and marry her while that fellow is still gaping at you. Then your poor mother can rest easy." Rest easy? Did she fear he was gay by any chance?

William smiled at this bizarre idea and also at the ingenuousness of the old man, maker of a safe middle-aged marriage himself. As if there were no more to it than that. As if it were so easy to be satisfied, to satisfy. He glanced up to where the others should be, but once again they had vanished into the mist that was perpetually forming and breaking above a certain height. At his level it was still warm and sunny but, looking back, he saw the sister mountain suspiciously close, as if it had taken several strides across the valley. It all meant rain, sooner or later. Maybe so late that they would be safely down and even on their way home by bus. Dermot and Rachel, unencumbered, might even be on top by now.

They were not, however. Breasting the next slope, William saw them waving to him. They were taking a rest, leaning up on their elbows in the heather. "Look over there for a change," William panted when he reached them at last, "and tell me what you see."

"The little mountain I climbed with the Hebrew group last year," Rachel said, pleased.

"I see rain," Dermot said, "but I don't see it soon. I may not even see it until we're all safe at home."

"That's what I think too," William agreed. "We could, of course, be wrong." He eased off the murderous rucksack and Rachel offered him her sympathy and, reaching into another pocket of the rucksack, some chocolate. They munched and complimented her on her foresight. Rachel blushed.

"My mother packed, actually – all of it," she said. "Just because I have five brothers and no sister, she thinks she has to keep on making up to me for something or other. I tell her if I had a sister we'd probably fight like cats, just like all the other sisters I knew in school, but she won't believe it. Says she never fought with *her* sisters."

"I never had anybody to fight with," William said, "I'm a child of aged parents."

"Accounts for his slightly neurotic attitude to normal things," Dermot said smoothly, "but he does the best he can. We mustn't blame him."

"So how many in *your* family, Dermot?" Rachel smiled. "You told me once but I've forgotten."

"Two brothers and a sister – all married, poor sods. Time we were moving on, friends. No place for dawdlers, this mountain."

"I'll carry my own rucksack for a while," Rachel, a little subdued, said to William. "It's ridiculous letting you carry everything."

"I'm used to the weight of it now," William said, "in fact I don't even feel it heavy. But thanks all the same."

"Like me to take it for a bit?" Dermot offered spuriously and was ignored.

This time William set the pace, proudly aware of the weight he was carrying, even pleased about it. He didn't look back or pause until, almost an hour later, he had reached the last stretch of loose boulders. By then he was right inside the cloud which billowed moistly around him. Looking back, he saw them a quarter of a mile away, Dermot fastening a scarf about Rachel's head, both of them wearing jerseys again.

From that point on the rain grew steadily heavier and the landscape was blotted out. He stooped to pick up a stone for the cairn, hoping Rachel was being duly warned about the danger of twisting her ankle, and that Dermot would not climb gallantly ahead of her to show her the way and send a couple of hundredweight of loose granite crashing into her knees. But he decided not to look back. Eyes closed against the stinging rain, he clambered blindly up. Simply, it was a job that had to be done. He knew this climb so well anyhow that he didn't need his eyes. When he reached the end of the boulders, half an hour later, the cairn was in sight, and then he did look back. Rachel was still on her feet at any rate, and Dermot had a hand on her spine, steering her up. Their heads were bent into the rain.

By the time they came shouting and dripping up the last few paces, he had a fire going, against all reason, and the shouts turned into cheers. They finally squatted around the fire together and Rachel unpacked the food. Into their frozen fingers she put rolls of fresh bread with a filling of savoury herring, and these were followed by pastry with chicken and mushrooms. William thought of the unknown woman whose guests, in a sense, they were. Rachel poured dry white wine into waxed paper cups, and by the time she had topped the picnic with Passover biscuits, there was Bewley's coffee for them in the billycan. It was hot, black and comforting, and Rachel was able to produce little lumps of sugar in paper packets – "I collect these whenever I go on a plane," she explained.

"You have absolutely no *idea* what it's like to look *down* on a waterfall," Dermot assured Rachel. "It should be over there. We'll come back again on a good day and I'll show you. It can't be described."

On the way down, Dermot told Rachel to go ahead while they found a tree. She nodded, and started off alone. Presently Dermot took William's arm and winked. "It will be too late for the last bus when we get down," he murmured. "Remember to back me. Our lone stand against the Age of the Automobile has its advantages, no?"

"I'm having no part in this," William heard himself saying in some surprise, "Jacob worked seven years if you remember for the other Rachel. Then seven more when her old man substituted the ugly sister. You've only known this Rachel for three months."

"Longer than I've known anybody else under similar frustrating conditions," Dermot leered amiably.

"Look," William pleaded, "she's Jewish, and an only daughter. Her decent mother packed all that lovely food for us. One of their prophets recommended the burning of girls who make love before marriage."

"The Jews have civilised themselves quite considerably since then," Dermot smiled. "Besides, they don't burn such girls now, there are too many of them. It would be wasteful, don't you think?"

"Leave her alone," William urged. "You've behaved like a fucking bastard often enough and will do again. Leave this one alone – she's not much more than a baby. Jewish girls live a more sheltered life than ours do, remember."

"Poor Jewish girls! Are you kidding?" Dermot laughed loudly, "Are you under the impression that *nobody* has ever made a serious pass at Rachel?"

"I'm suggesting nothing of the kind – after three months with you. But remember I know your cat and mouse games pretty well – she doesn't. If she did she probably wouldn't be here at all."

"Nevertheless you must credit her with the ability to decide her own fate for herself," Dermot said lightly, and launched himself on the downward track.

At the little pub, bright and warm in the surrounding darkness, they drank hot whiskey and lemon and Rachel seemed drowsy. Dermot ordered another round which Rachel sipped more slowly, unplaiting her hair between sips.

"How's the sore heel?" William asked her.

"I don't even notice it, thanks to you. You made a great job of it." Drowsily she smiled at him and he said, "It was nothing."

"On the contrary, it's what we bring him for, things like that," Dermot grinned.

"When will we be home, William?" It was perhaps a slight reproof to Dermot that the question was not addressed to him, but it was Dermot who answered anyway.

"No home for us tonight, love. Last bus has already gone, thanks to how slow we were in the rain. Not to worry, because they'll be able to put us up here snugly enough. And William has his American Express card, haven't you, William? How's the hair drying out?" He lifted up great golden handfuls into the firelight and let them go again. William's face was tickled by the downward fall and his nostrils teased by the steamy scented bathroom smell.

"Almost dry," Rachel sighed. "It's so warm in here." When Dermot put out an arm to her she settled back drowsily on to his shoulder but still smiled with the babyish teeth at William.

"Won't they be worrying about you at home?" William said stubbornly, ignoring Dermot's furious face above the girl's head. "They *are* expecting you home, aren't they?"

"Of course," Rachel said, shaking herself suddenly awake like a child. She stood up. "I must phone them. Excuse me."

"Wait," William heard himself saying, "It's not absolutely necessary to phone. Dermot's forgotten about the late bus that passes here from Wexford. It will have us in about half ten."

"He's deranged," Dermot drawled confidently. "Don't

listen to him, Rachel. That's the summer timetable he's thinking of, and it doesn't begin until next month."

"It began two weeks ago at Easter," William said levelly. "So take your choice, Rachel."

"Meanwhile I'll ask the curate if he *can* put us up," Dermot said smoothly. "Let William go if he pleases for the bus that I know won't come." Whistling, he rang the bell and the curate sidled in, then shook his head doubtfully at Dermot's question.

"I'll have to ask your woman inside," he said, vanishing.

"You can ask the curate when he comes back about the bus, too," William said quietly. "Before Rachel phones, perhaps?"

"I think I'd better phone now – just in case," Rachel said. It was obvious to Dermot that she had become uneasy. Dragging her climbing boots a little, muscles already stiffening even in the warmth, she loped over to the door and smiled a peculiar pacifying smile at both of them before going out.

"You have a fucking nerve," Dermot grated. "Playing God was never part of your act, remember?"

"Acts can change," William said. "Sometimes the second half is even better than the first. I'll take Rachel back on the bus myself if that's how she wants it."

"I have an odd feeling that's *not* how Rachel wants it," Dermot grinned, draining his whiskey. "Nothing more disappointing for God than when salvation is refunded, William, old pal."

"We'll see," said William.

Both their eyes were on the door. The curate sloped in first to say the boss had said it was O.K. if the two men would share a room, and then they waited, glaring at one another, for the scrape of Rachel's boots on the tiles outside.

Phone You Some Time

It's a funny thing about Dublin. Small though it is, a village almost in some ways, you will never meet anybody you want to meet by accident. You will hear news of him. You will meet a cousin of his. You will talk to people who have just left him in a pub not more than an hour ago. But you will never under any circumstances meet him accidentally in the street.

I know because I tried so often to do it, that summer that belonged jointly to Stephen and Jean Marc. I spent much of it in the company of Jean Marc thinking about Stephen. The trouble was that nothing had really ended with Stephen. The last thing he said to me was, "Phone you some time," and for months I believed he would. Alone (if you don't count my father) among my globe-trotting family I was determined to spend the long college vacation right here in Dublin, most of the time in reach of the telephone. I wasn't going to be caught napping in New York like my sister or in Germany like my engineer brothers when that bloody phone rang at last. I wasn't even going to be in West Cork with my mother watching her lick the local dramatic society into shape for the winter season. That Little Theatre reverently supported her the whole summer long for what they believed she could do for them – had she not, in her youth, had "the voice Shakespeare dreamed off when he created Juliet?" That of course was a long time ago and the drama critic who said it was silent at last under a handsome marble tomb-stone in Glasnevin, but his words lived on in a gilt frame on our living-room wall, and West Cork remembered.

No, I wasn't going to West Cork and I wasn't going to give English lessons in Paris or to work in the kitchens of

Germany. I wasn't going anywhere because I knew Stephen wasn't either. He was repeating a failed exam in September. My family seized on me delightedly when the letter arrived from Jean Marc's mother.

"The *sweet* Vendrons," my family sighed, but I knew exactly what was coming. We had all stayed at one time or another with the sweet Vendrons in Marseilles for the purpose of improving our French, and they in turn had stayed with us. Jean Marc had come as a shy silent schoolboy of fifteen. He had come the year after his sister Amelie, a creature of such overpowering beauty and wit that for several summers afterwards we were plagued with phonecalls from hopeful boys in the neighbourhood – Amelie just *might* perhaps be staying with us again? Thank God she never did stay again. My family would not have survived it. We always hoped however for another visit from her older sister Françoise, who radiated delight in the most ordinary daily routine of our lives and who learned English with a rapidity that astonished us and caused her family to send us their problem, Jean Marc, the only son, with hopes that proved misplaced.

His second visit was somehow unexpected by everybody but me. The most elementary common sense would have told them that the only one of the Vendrons who *needed* to come again was Jean Marc, since he had gone home at the end of the summer practically as ignorant of the English language as when he arrived. That was because his suitcase had been stuffed with French novels which he read all the time when he wasn't tuned in to ORTF on his little transistor.

Now he was coming back again accompanied by three cases of his father's best wine and an urgent appeal from his mother. He had no academic future and needed absolutely fluent English to manage his father's business affairs in England. That was the future that had been mapped out for him at twenty, after he had made two unsuccessful attempts to gain his Bac.

It took my mother practically no time at all to decide

that Jean Marc would be happiest of all with me and my father. He was a shy boy and families tended to overwhelm him, my mother said. It wasn't that they couldn't have made different plans for the summer if they'd known in time about Jean Marc, but as it was – well, it might turn out for the best. After all, I'd *wanted* to stay at home anyway.

Jean Marc arrived, to a choice of three empty bedrooms. My mother, guiltily attentive on the eve of her own departure, had prepared a dazzling array of cold dishes for his delight but Jean Marc (taller and heavier now but looking no older) wasn't hungry. He felt sick from the flight and thought he would like to go straight to bed. It was eight o'clock on a summer's evening, and he was twenty years old, like me. He wanted to go to bed.

"He's rather big and coarse in comparison with the rest of his family, but he is better-looking now," my mother said uneasily. "Besides, he seemed to understand us much better than he used to."

"I was speaking French," I pointed out.

"Then you had better stop speaking French," my mother said indignantly. "He's here to learn – finally – to speak English. Not a word of French to him from this out."

I am the only one she can bully still and she enjoys it. It has always been like that. My father (retired now from his Government office) and I are the only people in the family who can be counted on to have nothing to do. We have certain useful skills, like driving, however, on which the rest of the family can confidently depend.

Next day I drove my mother to Cork before Jean Marc was awake, and in Cork she was met by an old friend who would drive her the rest of the way. On the road back I wondered for a crazy twenty miles or so what would happen if I didn't bother going home at all. It was mid-June and the car roof was open. The smells of haymaking came up to me from the fields and the macadam road was dark blue in the sunlight. Somewhere west was a dazzling coastline where we had all spent childhood holidays.

Somewhere south was an old harbour where I had friends, where one could lie on hot cobblestones in the sun and talk to fishermen and dream of being there with Stephen. Somewhere there was an end of responsibility to other people which I seemed to have shouldered long before I left school because I was the dull one in a bright family. I knew that responsibility to my mother for Jean Marc, to my cheerful pottering father, to Jean Marc himself, and to the heap of old brick and ruined outhouses that was our home, was not something which I could shrug off because it seemed to have been part of my consciousness for so long. My only concession to a wanton impulse was to stop at a dark little country pub for a glass of lager and listen as I drank it to the publican's story of how he once went to Dublin one blazing summer's day long ago. He went to have his gall-bladder X-rayed, and I was given an account of it, blow by blow.

It was evening when I got in, and the only evidence of Jean Marc was the shuttered rooms downstairs. That's a thing I've noticed about the French – they hate sunlight indoors. What I remembered about Jean Marc's own home in Marseilles was the coolness of the dark rooms when you stepped in out of blazing sunlight. In the hall there was a floor of polished stone that would not have been out of place in an old church, and in the room where his family ate there was a chill green light from the half-closed shutters that made you fancy you were in an aquarium.

Going from room to room, I let in the sunshine, thick and golden now as honey at half past seven in the evening. The faint humming of a dynamo from the bottom of the garden spoke of my father's presence, but where was Jean Marc? On my way to my own room I noticed that the door of his was half-open, but there was no sign of him until I got down to the kitchen a while afterwards. He was sitting at the wide-open window shredding carrots, with evidence of coleslaw all around him. Newly-made mayonnaise was in a brown bowl on the table in the corner now set for three. Jean Marc was smiling, dark teeth in a broad brown face. One of the front teeth was badly filled with gold. He walked like a snake (but then so do all French boys) across the kitchen to find a pepper mill. I suddenly saw that somebody might some day find him attractive.

"*You* did all this, Jean Marc?"

"Monsieur helped me by telling me where everything was." He spoke in rapid southern French in reply to my English.

"But he was to take you out to eat because I wasn't here!"

"We decided we preferred to eat at home. Madame has left so much food already prepared," Jean Marc said shyly. "Besides, I like to cook."

He chose a light and sparkling rosé from one of the cases his father had sent, and my father looked smug when summoned from the garden. All his days now, like all his office holidays long ago, were spent playing with old cars. He had never come away on holidays with us in his life. He also hated restaurants.

"A nice way you took Jean Marc out to dinner!" I accused him.

"He likes to cook, don't you, Jean Marc?"

"I like to cook," the boy nodded, and I noted with pleasure that he liked to eat too. Less shy than last time, he still never initiated any conversation but he responded to anybody else's remarks and he didn't look as unhappy as when he arrived. He persistently answered me in French though he made an effort at English with my father, whose knowledge of French was limited to what one finds about motoring in old phrase books.

"How's the head?" said my father, helping himself to the excellent mayonnaise his guest had produced, and I felt ashamed at having forgotten how ill Jean Marc had seemed on arrival.

"Your headache," I translated for him. "Is it any better?"

"Mais oui," Jean Marc shrugged it off, and then smiled darkly as he poured wine for us. How had he missed the dazzling white teeth the rest of his family had been blessed with? He first passed the bottle to my father, then yielded to the host's gesture. It was, after all, *his* wine, made by *his* father and uncles, bottled by them, shipped all over Europe. Its label was respected everywhere except perhaps in England. Jean Marc's mission was to foster it there and for this we had to provide him with the language.

"Did you choose to go into the business?" I asked him afterwards.

"Ma mère a choisi," Jean Marc said, with no strong implication of criticism. Yes – his mother decided most things for the family. Of course.

It was several days later before the subject came up again. It was in the garden one day after lunch. "I want to escape," he said. Just that. "I tell you this because you look like Gabrielle."

"Gabrielle?"

Great plump pigeons picked around fearlessly at the remains of our lunch and I saw with astonishment that Jean Marc's round brown eyes were full of tears. My father had gone back to his ancient engines as soon as he could gobble down the cold meal, but before he left us he said to Jean Marc, "You're one of the family – I don't have to remember the formalities." Now Jean Marc was saying I looked like Gabrielle and his eyes were full of tears and he was one of the family.

"Gabrielle?" I asked him sympathetically, but it was a long time before he answered. When he did it was in an ordinary voice and his eyes had been shaken dry, like a dog's coat. I might even have imagined his distress, but I knew I hadn't.

"Gabrielle and I were friends," he mumbled. "What I must say is that she regarded herself as my friend but I was in love with her. She was also a friend of Amelie."

"Ah, Amelie," I said lamely.

"I may tell you?" Jean Marc said gently, and then I knew I must have looked so abstracted that, scrupulously polite like all his family, he had detected possible boredom.

"Tell me, please."

It was hot in the garden, and the circle of shade where we sat under the apple tree was narrowing. The old engine my father was working on spluttered feebly into life and died again. The pigeons were gone and an army of sparrows was cleaning up what remained. In the shade, they flurried like brown butterflies, on the edge of consciousness.

"She was a friend of your sister Amelie who stayed here?" Brilliant beautiful overpowering Amelie.

"She is at the university with Françoise and came home a few times to eat with us in the evening. She and Amelie played guitar together afterwards. Later Gabrielle played sometimes with me."

The image of the explosive Amelie quietly playing guitar duets with another girl somehow didn't tally with the man-eater we had known, but one had to wait for the end of the story. "When you said Gabrielle was like me, you meant physically?" I prompted, and Jean Marc nodded.

"Long hair straight like yours and almost the same brown. Blue eyes and blue shirt like yours," Jean Marc said innocently. He sighed, rolled over on the grass and was quiet for a long time. Maybe after all it was only a French-made shirt we had in common?

"We went to concerts and to the open-air theatre at Avignon once and then she was to come grape-picking for my father – I also – in September. She did not come."

"Why?"

He rolled over again and didn't look at me. "Because Amelie was tired of her friend Jean-Claude. She had begun to see somebody else. Jean-Claude had to repeat an examination in the autumn and my mother warned Amelie she must not make him unhappy. So –" He stopped speaking again and the sound was filled up with the wheezy protests of my father's newest old car.

"I know what happened. You needn't finish. La belle Amelie introduced Jean-Claude to Gabrielle and you didn't see Gabrielle any more?"

"D'accord." He looked profoundly gloomy now. "Jean-Claude has a sports car and a great deal of money to spend. Me, no. I had to save for eight weeks to take her to Avignon by train."

This I could well imagine. The richer people's parents are, very often the less money changes hands. Poor Jean Marc. I recognised the compliment to me for what it was – an impulse of loneliness. "I tell you this because you look like Gabrielle." Tant pis. Even if he meant it, I was not for him any more than Stephen was for me. Each one of us is isolated in his own deficiencies. But to distract him a little I took him on a tour of my father's private empire.

I suppose this annexe to our house must seem extraordinary to somebody who doesn't know it. The house itself is on the southern outskirts of Dublin quite close to the foothills that border Wicklow. It was once an old farmhouse, in no way distinguished and quite small before various pieces were built on. But the point is that the old cobbled farmyard still remains around at the back together with most of the crumbling outhouses.

It was certainly the reason why my father bought the house in the first place. At that time it was isolated and very cheap. Now speculative builders have gradually crept up almost to the edge of the farmyard itself, or rather, to the other side of the screen of poplars. A whole new wilderness of housing is on all sides of us, and for most of ten years now my mother had been urging my father to sell out and make a fortune. Sell out? He'd rather sell her and us and all our furniture than budge from his rest-home for old cars. Did he not found it? Endow it with his perpetual care and most of his money over the years? Were the unsavoury-looking medley of wrecked automobiles not his friends as well as his charges? Did they not time and again delight him by offering him sufficient parts that fitted sweetly together to form a workable whole?

Where once heavy farm horses had been groomed and fed, where once chickens had roosted and golden harvests had been gathered, there the old cars settled to end their days, each one a gem of its own kind to my father, each possessed of a human charm and personality, so that he went around frowning for days on the occasions when somebody came to buy something from him – whether it was a spare part that could be found in no other place in the city or a reconstituted wreck that was capable of being driven (by my father) around the farmyard and that *somebody*, young, usually, and mad, thought of as being a practically free passport to the car-owning classes.

My father was always much more willing to lend than to sell. He didn't mind so much selling a part, but selling a car he had created out of the bodies of his friends was to him a sacrilege. Once when he met his match in a determined man who came every day for three weeks with ever-increasing offers for a Riley Gamecock, he finally agreed to sell it for £350, only on condition that its owner would never sell it to anybody but himself when its usefulness was at an end. He had the legal agreement hanging up for years on the kitchen wall.

Anyway, it was my mother's habit to pretend the Cars' Graveyard, as she called it, didn't exist at all, and we had been ordered since childhood never to show it to a visitor. Jean Marc, however, was one of the family. My father had said so, and fortunately my mother was away. So I took him through the rose garden, which made me think of beautiful Stephen again, and around to the back. In the late afternoon light my father was nowhere to be seen, but his family was everywhere – dusty, dilapidated, but trustfully crouched in stable and barn ready for the revivifying touch that he might at any time give them. They only had to wait. If you looked at the place another way it was just a scrap yard, and the French are tidy to a fault.

"Mais c'est bizarre, ça," Jean Marc smiled, and when he smiled his gold tooth winked cheerfully in the sun. You forgot that his round brown eyes had ever been full of tears.

"You see – it's our horrible secret. Last time you stayed with us my mother absolutely forbade us to show it to you."

"My father," he said admiringly, "would not dare!"

"You mean he'd like to support a million geriatric cars as well as his wife and family?"

The complexity of this English sentence defeated Jean Marc. He laughed, shook his head, edged sideways into an outhouse, then climbed in his impeccably neat (in fact square) blue jeans into the dusty ruins of a clover-leaf Citröen. "In France," he said, "they would pay you in gold bars for this one. Que c'est beau!"

As we both sat in the fragile glove-leather front seats, I became aware of voices on the other side of us – most probably from the barn. There was my father's high voice lecturing on the beauties of some particular wreck and there was this other voice that made my blood race and my knees tremble. I was glad I was sitting down. I couldn't believe it – maybe I was delirious? How could it possibly be Stephen's voice? I *was* delirious. It couldn't be.

Jean Marc became suddenly concerned for my health. "Vous vous sentez bien?" he asked anxiously, and I became aware for the first time how kind his rough-skinned brown face was. He was looking at me with the tenderness my father reserved for the most aristocratic and touchingly beautiful of his wrecked cars.

"Jean Marc, will you do something for me?"

"Of course. If it is possible for me."

"Pretend – oh, pretend I really *am* Gabrielle when we go in to find my father. Will you?"

Jean Marc laughed uncomfortably. He had by now become aware of the voices too.

"But if you were, I would not sit with you here like this. I could not say a word. I would knock things over and stammer and behave so stupidly she would – she would –" He trailed off and shrugged hopelessly and I was afraid he was going to cry again.

"Look, Jean Marc, just *pretend*, can't you? I am Gabrielle but I do not think you could ever behave stupidly. I think it was a beautiful thing to save up enough money to take me to the Festival of Avignon and I think you are very sweet. Which, as a matter of fact, I do."

"D'accord, allons," Jean Marc said, quite suddenly a different person. I was to learn before the summer was out that he was happiest of all when given something positive to do which he *knew* was very useful to somebody.

My father was extremely embarrassed when we appeared, and dived hurriedly under a car. Stephen was not embarrassed at all. Taller even than I remembered, and slimmer, he was dressed in elegantly faded blue levis and a matching shirt of pure silk. He was blonder and more positively superior to anybody else I'd ever known. He still looked at you directly between the brows with a childlike candour of pale blue eyes and his golden beard was bright in the sun. He was not in the least put out.

"How are you, Felicity?" he smiled. "How delightful to see you again."

Jean Marc's hand over mine tightened sweatily in the heat. He was so much bigger and clumsier than Stephen that he seemed to exude heat as much as Stephen made you think of cool smart bars. But the brown arm of Jean Marc came firmly around my waist and was not even taken aback when he offered the other hand to Stephen.

"This is – well, some time you'll have to know anyway – this is Jean Marc from Marseilles," I said cunningly. The warm arm firmly around my waist and its tightened fingers gave me confidence. My legs didn't give way any more.

"Are you by any chance Amelie's brother?"

"Yes," said Jean Marc in English.

"Ah," said Stephen with an unflattering glance from the square Spanish sandals to the coarse dark hair of Jean Marc. He didn't need to say, "How *could* an oaf like you be the brother of such a beautiful girl?" Jean Marc understood perfectly but he didn't flinch even when his outstretched brown hand was left dangling.

"You will perhaps excuse us," he said with a practically unprecedented command of English. "Felicité and I go for a meal this evening to town. We must perhaps change."

This was, I thought, magnificent. It even gave my father courage to emerge from under the antiquated Morris 8, the sort of car which he said the pre-war English misguidedly referred to as a "sports tourer."

"I did wonder," I said with a wild stab in the dark, "when you might end a visit to the Graveyard by dropping in to the house. You've been coming to talk my father into selling this – this vehicle for quite a while, haven't you, Stephen?"

"It *is* rather difficult to part Mr Power from any of his showpieces," he admitted, and laughed with admirably contrived naturalness. "I'd intended, of course, to let you know when the bargain was happily struck – which, as a matter of fact, I do believe it is now."

"Do you now?" my father said, straightening up at last and looking me in the eye. "Do you now?"

Stephen couldn't possibly have known it, but my father was looking extremely wicked indeed. His tufted white hair gave him the air of a surprised swan and his eyes had an abstracted innocence we had all learned to distrust long ago. His face was grease-marked and he rubbed a grubby paw across his brow which temporarily darkened a tuft of the ridiculous hair.

"Well, I thought –" Stephen shrugged, but he wasn't nearly so self-possessed as he wanted to appear. He was looking worried, as well he might.

"Come back next summer when I've had time to work on her a bit more then we'll see. I just *might* sell her to you," my father said expansively, "if we made a signed agreement that you'd never sell her – to anybody but me, that is."

That old trick again! Jean Marc tried to pull me away to prepare for that mythical meal, but I couldn't have budged. I was trying to analyse why I didn't feel sorry for Stephen – not a bit.

"But sir –" Stephen protested, as my father raised an overpowering greasy paw.

"That's enough. Come in for a drink and welcome but

don't mention Annabel to me until June of next year."

"Phone you some time," Stephen muttered to nobody in particular and walked away across the cobblestones with what dignified languor he could muster. We watched him disappear in the direction of the bus.

Then my father sat down on the running-board of a 1936 Railton and laughed. He has a wheezy maddening laugh that can go on for days, and I wasn't amused now.

"It's unethical," I said indignantly, and shook off Jean Marc's arm because he was laughing too – loudly, and I'd never heard him laugh before. "You led him on like the wicked old man you are and you had no intention of selling him this – this Annabel or whatever you call it. Don't deny it."

"She," said my father. "Miss Annabel Morris, if you please," and then he went on laughing. "I'd intended of course to let you know when the bargain was actually struck," he mimicked with unpardonable accuracy, "which as a matter of fact I do believe it is now –" The tears poured down his face, making grease-tracks as they ran. Then suddenly he stopped and said to me, "*He* didn't mind how he led you on."

I was about to go back into the house, completely exasperated with myself because by his behaviour my father had made me feel sorry for Stephen despite myself, when I became aware of the deflated Jean Marc. Big hands by his sides, he looked dispossessed again, awkward, his usefulness at an end. As often happens, my father was aware of the deflated Jean Marc at exactly the same moment I was myself. He became suddenly businesslike and got to his feet.

"You were splendid, Jean Marc," I said, rushing to congratulate him. "You convinced even me."

"Come here, Jean Marc," my father said.

"Sir?"

"Can you drive? Have you a driving licence?"

"Certainly, sir."

"Hop in and show me. You too, Felicity. First, I'll show

you the gears," he said to Jean Marc, "because I don't suppose you've driven anything with only three gears before, and if you put her into reverse by mistake and catapult yourselves through the windscreen, I might find it quite hard to get another unscratched one."

This particular Morris 8, a spidery little two-seater newly graduated to the ranks of "veteran," was more beautiful than its designer could have hoped. My father had painted her a ravishing olive-green outside and worked her mushroom leather upholstery to a fine gloss and softness. Her brasses gleamed prettily, and it was no wonder Stephen had thought her ready. In a few moments Jean Marc had manoeuvred her gently out of the big barn and we were purring around the farmyard to the accompaniment of approving noises from my father.

"Handled as sweetly as I'd use her myself, boy – very good. Excellent. Brakes are a bit sharp until the linings wear in. O.K. Right. I'll tell you this much – Felicity couldn't handle her so gently, could you now?"

"Whatever you say," I murmured, but I was beginning to get the glimmer of the idea that might be moving around inside his tufted head.

"What I need is somebody I can trust to drive her at least a few hundred miles and see how she measures up, what's still to do. What do you say, Jean Marc?"

He didn't understand, so I translated for him and he giggled, round brown eyes glistening with pleasure.

"Felicity will go with you and show you the west coast or wherever you like. Do me a favour, boy, and give Annabel a trial."

Once again, for the second time in the same afternoon, Jean Marc felt needed and he looked at me questioningly in speechless happiness.

"Ça va?" I asked him.

"Ça va," he said fervently, and so unpropitiously began the education of Jean Marc in the English language. It was almost the last bit of French spoken on that gloriously successful holiday on which the sun shone, day after day, while we toured the country at a suitably dignified forty miles an hour. In the villages through which we passed, people stood to watch the beauty of Annabel, to smile sentimentally at Jean Marc and me. When we went in for a beer in little country pubs, the men came out to examine Father's treasure before we set off again, and in Mullingar Jean Marc shouted out his first spontaneous words of English to a countryman whose pony was about to back into our car.

"Please, please, attention!"

"We say, 'Be careful!' " I muttered.

Jean Marc got out anxiously onto the road. "*Please* be careful, sir," he shouted, and the man whipped his horse into stillness, climbed down off his cart, and stood beside Jean Marc to examine our remarkable car.

"She's a beauty, that one right enough," he said, tilting the cap back on his head. "When the brother came over from the States in '36 he hired a little machine the dead spit of herself. Ye have her lovely, so ye have."

Not understanding a word of all this, Jean Marc stood by smiling and the countryman wished us good luck and stood holding the reins of his pony while Jean Marc manoeuvred Annabel carefully out of the crowded main street of Mullingar.

I said the sun shone for the whole of that holiday and so it nearly did. It shone in Killybegs and in Connemara, where Jean Marc caught a flat fish with his bare hands and cooked it in country butter on the little primus stove my father had given us. It shone on the glittering hide of the Shannon at Killaloe, and it shone on the little fishing villages I had dreamed of showing to Stephen. But in Youghal there was one shower of summer rain and we ran dripping from the harbour to the waiting shelter of Annabel's ridiculous canvas hood – my father had still some happy work ahead where that was concerned – where she was parked in Market Dock, and inside we laughed and carefully mopped her mushroom leather seats with our towels before we dried ourselves.

"If you were Gabrielle I would not dare to make love to you," Jean Marc said in English, correctly, just like that.

"I am Felicity, and all Gabrielle and I have in common is one blue French shirt," I said firmly, and that was the beginning of Jean Marc's determination to extend his father's business to Ireland.

At home again, my father insisted on selling Annabel to Jean Marc for £10, one quarter of his holiday pocket money, on condition that he only used her in Ireland and garaged her with us. "That will be perfectly agreeable, since eventually I shall live in Dublin," said Jean Marc confidently, and now when he phones from London, where he's happily learning the business, he always asks about Annabel's health. There's no need for phone watching – Jean Marc rings promptly at ten o'clock every Sunday.

A Summer in London

IT HAD been Eleanor's idea and she had described this orgy in Harrods very well. Her mother had taken her there after the exams on her annual shopping spree in London last year. Eleanor had described the breeze billowing through white tulle curtains, the starched tablecloths, the pianist playing Palm Court music with liberal use of the soft pedal, the air of slothful luxury in the middle of London on an ordinary Tuesday afternoon.

But no words her friends remembered could have done justice to the flower-filled altar itself. They had clutched one another and fallen around laughing at the looped white linen, the trailing Victorian garlands of leaves, the fresh flowers which garnished the table on which were spread out hundreds of sugar confections. There were meringues of every colour and shape, cherry cakes and chocolate cakes and Battenburg cakes, there were fluffy dark devil's food cakes with sugar violets on top and strawberry flans stiff with cream and of course there were chocolate eclairs and every imaginable kind of bun. Neither Una nor Catherine could believe that all you had to do once a waitress had found you a table was take one or two plates from it and go off to collect your own loot. Once the £5 had been paid in advance (only £3.75 last year, Eleanor had said) you could pick and choose as you might in your own flower garden. There were the befrilled waitresses and boys in white coats to help you to things which needed cutting such as large cartwheels of Black Forest cherry cake in kirsch and gateaux which looked like something which might have been served to Marie Antoinette in the Petit Trianon. Catherine giggled nervously as she remembered the rigidity of the diet she had followed before deciding to come to London on a summer job.

"Don't think about it," Eleanor kindly advised, "just enjoy it. We won't come again."

"Not if we are to save £150 each in six weeks and stay alive at the same time," Una said, grimly.

"Relax," Eleanor said. She had a self-indulgent mother who encouraged the celebration of practically everything. It was easy for her. "I'm not taking a penny from either of you," Eleanor smiled. "This is just something I want to treat us all to. So just let's be hogs and enjoy it or I'll wish I hadn't been such a fool."

Giggling as though they were back at school again, they heaped up their plates as the pianist put his soft-pedal foot down again and played "You Will Remember Vienna." Back at their table they eyed one another's plates and giggled again. White curtains puffed out behind them like bridal veils.

"Two cream horns seems a bit ambitious," Una said.

"Don't worry, there won't be a single crumb left," said Eleanor. But there was more. There was a whole cream horn left on her plate when she finally admitted defeat. Una had eaten her way through everything, however (although she kept saying that what she would really like was a heap of raw grated carrot), and Catherine had left half an eclair. Eleanor poured more tea for them all and the pianist tinkled on. "I keep wondering why anybody comes alone to a place like this," Eleanor said softly at last, nodding towards a huge lady in a pink straw hat whose face was red from effort.

"She's come alone every Friday for fifteen years since her best friend who was at school with her died," invented Catherine. "They lived in Croyden and always came by train to shop at the Food Hall every Friday. Afternoon tea up here was their little treat for the week. Her friend was called Rose and she is Ivy."

"I think it's obscene," Una shuddered. "They all look so greedy. Every time more cakes are carried in some of them go up again. That little thin man (how does he do it?) with the panama hat and the buttonhole – he's up and down like a Jack-in-the-box."

"I think he's sweet," said Eleanor. "He only goes up to look. Mostly he doesn't take anything else."

"I suppose it keeps them out of the pubs," Una decided at last. "That's about all you can say in its favour. All that money for junk food!"

"Saying that is hardly a polite response to an invitation that I for one think is fun and am thoroughly enjoying. I'll always remember the way we spent our first afternoon together in London." Catherine was nothing if not mannerly. They hadn't in fact known one another very well in college – not well enough for that sort of frankness anyhow. It had simply happened that they had discovered they were all going to London for the same reason and might as well keep in touch. Catherine ended her civil speech by smiling happily at Eleanor who in turn looked relieved.

"It was different when I came with Mother last year. She remembered it from the fifties, you see, when she and my father chose London for their honeymoon. She kept telling me about the string orchestra which used to play and the starched table napkins and the fifty different kinds of scone alone you could choose from and the special flowery dresses all the women wore. It cost 5/- then, I think, and my father said he could live here. Which didn't surprise me to hear because Mother admitted she wooed him with Bewley's coffee and chocolate biscuits in Ranelagh."

"He wouldn't live long on this diet," Una stuck sourly to her guns, "nor deserve to. Are you all ready?"

"He's alive and well thank you and devoted at other times of the day to yoghurt and steak and coleslaw," said Eleanor, with a broad smile.

In a way, it was like pulling themselves out of a fairy tale but they got their belongings together at last and surfaced. The Barcarolle from 'The Tales of Hoffman' followed them softly out into the furniture department. Catherine sat down suddenly on one of the creaking wicker chairs.

"I think I'm going to be sick," she said, and looked it.

"I know where the loo is – quick!" said Eleanor and led the way. Catherine could unfortunately be heard being sick and she looked surprised when she emerged from the lavatory.

They didn't see one another again for a week, and then only because Eleanor phoned the other two. She was working as a chambermaid in a central London hotel called 'The Sir Roger' because Addison was reputed to have stayed there for several years. It was now long past its prime except for the hall which still looked like the entrance to a comfortable country house. The dining-room and the room still marked "Drawing Room" had brightly polished brasses and a lot of old mahogany. Several castor oil plants had somehow survived since the days when they were last fashionable and now, in vogue again, they were a sumptuous contrast to the plastic flower arrangements of more modern and more expensive hotels. But as you progressed lower down or higher up into the house the place degenerated into the ruin it really was. Untreated dry rot had mushrooms sprouting evilly all over the larders and kitchens. The sound of rats scampering and foraging at night frequently frightened away new male staff who were expected to sleep tumbled together in strange cell-like places reeking of damp. Upstairs the damp from missing slates and uncleaned gutters made the old wallpaper billow and ooze, the paint crumble away.

The worst bedrooms of all were under the roof of the house where the female staff slept five or six to a room. In heavy rain you had to catch the drips in plastic buckets and if you forgot to empty them in time the floods met you on your way up to bed. The manager only worried when the water seeped down into the guest rooms on the fourth floor.

Eleanor had been adaptable since childhood and kept telling herself she was lucky to have a job in the very heart of London. The rest of the housemaids and chambermaids were all right to work with if not very comfortable to sleep with, and the only thing she found intolerable was the heat of the linen room where she spent most of every day. She had to collect changes of linen there, put away the stuff just back from the laundry and do the ironing. The housekeeper was particular about the appearance of the shelves in case the manager should ever choose to look in but she wasn't particular about changing the linen after one-night stays. Part of Eleanor's job was to iron used sheets so that they looked new when put back on the beds. After one night's use, however, they were only topped and tailed for the next guest, and ironed for the third. As soon as they began to be noticeably unfresh, however, Eleanor had to make sure they went to be laundered. She began to know the look of guests whose linen would not survive to be used again and it amused her (however clean they might look) to be proved right.

It was one of the few amusements of her job. The heat in the linen room was so overpowering (because it was directly over the main boiler) that she often had to remove her dress and work in bra and knickers with sweat pouring from her. Mrs Ledmore was furious the first time she discovered the new chambermaid thus divested but she stopped complaining the day Eleanor passed out with the heat and had to be revived with cold face cloths and an extravagant sip of brandy.

The three girls met next time in the coffee bar of the National Gallery one pouring wet afternoon in July. Eleanor was crying to the dismay of the others and they wondered what had happened to her determined cheerfulness of just a week ago. Catherine tried to make her laugh by dumping on her plate a tiny thing like a grass snake. She said she had tended it from a seedling and looked after it like a mother.

"What is it?" Eleanor managed to ask, blowing her nose and then quickly putting away her handkerchief.

"It's going to be a courgette," said Catherine, "or rather if I'd not uprooted it, that's what it would be. All its family are courgettes." She worked for a market gardener in Kent and made fifty pounds a week. By living in a hostel she might save twenty pounds a week, or even more.

Una asked bluntly what was wrong with Eleanor. Crying never solved anything. Catherine tried to hush her, but it was too late. "Kevin is here in London," Eleanor said at last. "He came to see me yesterday at the hotel." Tears began to pour down her face again but no sound came.

"I know exactly what's wrong with you," Una said. "He's upset you by raising objections. Your mind was made up, and now it isn't."

"Exactly," Eleanor agreed, and took out her handkerchief again. This time she dried her face and no more tears came but she drew in a couple of very deep breaths. "He says he doesn't want me to do it. Says if I do it the odds are I may never have another child – this *happens,* he says – and anyhow, it's *ours,* not just mine. I should see it, he says, and so should he, and then we should decide if we can go through with adoption."

"Is he staying in London?" Una wanted to know.

"Just for two days on his way to Holland. He'll be working there until October."

"Easy for him to be sentimental, isn't it?" Una said savagely. "*His* baby for God's sake! Why don't you give it to him now and let him carry it the rest of the way?"

They all laughed. Eleanor drank a glass of milk and decided to be cheerful again. "I half agree with him, you know. Maybe I never will have another child. Maybe it would have been brilliant and beautiful. James Stephens was a bastard and so was Sarah Bernhardt. You just have to do nothing once the thing starts, and then you have a baby. You don't have to say, 'Today I'll make its legs and tomorrow its brains.' You have to do nothing but eat properly and stay sane and then in nine months you have a baby that's like no other in the world and that's yours for ever and his. Always biologically yours and his whoever may rear it."

"Stop it, stop it!" Una said. "All the reasons for which you came to London are still valid. You don't WANT a baby, you never asked for one, and your life will be ruined if you go ahead. Quite simply you were a careless fool like everybody else and you're pregnant. Happily it's reversible."

Catherine had been playing with the courgette. "I see what she means, though. You can't help thinking along those lines when you work in my job. Growth itself is a fascination. Especially the private growth in your own body which takes other people so long to notice."

"Not all *that* long," said Una grimly. "Do nothing and they'll notice soon enough. And then at that stage the whole business is grisly and I can understand why nurses hate it. But none of that need happen in our cases. I've already made arrangements (God be good to you Marie Stopes!) for July 20th. I'd thought both of you would have done the same by now."

"I have," Eleanor said quickly, "July 28th is my date. It's just that I'm not sure any more."

"Nor am I," Catherine said, "even although I was delighted last week when I got the result of the examination and the signatures of the two doctors. I was absolutely *certain* then that I was doing the only sensible thing in the circumstances. But that was last week . . ." Her voice trailed off on a sigh.

Una shook her head in exasperation. "I simply don't believe what I'm hearing. How would you BOTH have felt if the doctors had refused to refer you and you were stuck? Have you the remotest idea of what rearing a child on your own means? My sister . . ."

"Please," said Eleanor, "we know all the arguments. It's just that I'm no longer sure I want to do it."

"My mother, for instance," said Catherine, "would probably love to have a child running around the house again."

"I wouldn't bank on it," Una said grimly. "Empty nest syndrome is all very well at one level. At another the woman wouldn't be human if she wasn't actually glad that all the donkey-work was over. Beginning all over again in late middle age because your daughter has been an imbecile wouldn't be everybody's cup of tea and maybe not your mother's. You didn't tell her anyway."

"Only because I knew her views on abortion. The bishops have told her what to think and she takes their word for it. Murder!"

"A few pregnant bishops would alter everything in a remarkably short time. Roll on the ordination of women, I say."

It was still raining after tea so they wandered around the Flemish rooms which seemed to be full of pregnant women, on the walls or looking at them. During a break in the rain they all walked to Oxford Street with Catherine who wanted to buy a blurry print dress full enough to allow for growth while she saved her money and suitable in design for being glimpsed amid the apple trees. Catherine was inclined to be romantic.

She smiled to herself over this as she clutched the parcel from Selfridges on her way back by underground to her village. She had to get a bus when the line petered out at last among the straggling fields and on the bus she felt queasy. To distract her mind she thought of the baby after seven weeks growth, trying to remember the photographs she had seen as a twelve-year-old gaining instruction. Somewhere inside that weird shape were the genes and chromosomes which would give it male or female sex, brown eyes or blue, fine dark hair like her own or rough brown curly hair like Brendan's, even perhaps a way of clearing its throat like her father's, or a tendency to walk with toes turned in like her mother's. She wondered if anything could change a pre-ordained order at this stage, as more or less light could change the contours of a plant. She had lulled herself to such a state of amused calm that she wasn't sick this time and the sight of Brendan waiting in the dusk at the bus stop was merely a miracle she had half expected. They had parted on bad terms and he had called her irresponsible and careless. Now he was the old affectionate joking Brendan once again who had, it seemed found a job not too far away, in the hop fields. He assumed she'd had the abortion already and hoped she would share a room with him over a little pub. She would, and suddenly she felt cheerful for the first time in many weeks. She'd made up her mind. No point in complicating everything by being stupidly stubborn at this stage. She'd phone Una tomorrow.

Una had the softest job of the three, with her own Laura Ashley-style bedroom at the back of a mews house off Kensington High Street. When she looked out from her window she could see past the spire of St Mary Abbot's along the green sward of Kensington Gardens to the fountains. Because of the trees the traffic sounds were muffled. In the mornings she took the children out walking, and after lunch she gave pre-school lessons to the older child while the younger one was having his nap. Una disliked children on the whole but found Emma and Andrew bearable. Their doctor parents had trained them to be amiable with a variety of strangers who had cared for them since birth. Una was responsible for preparing a simple lunch for herself and the children but a woman who came in the afternoons cooked dinner, usually a good one. When the parents were staying in the city Una had to see the children to bed and was supposed to read to them. But in fact the cook, who had grandchildren of her own, often did that and Una escaped to the park or out for a drink with the Arab student she had met at a pop concert in the Albert Hall. She was punctilious about being back in time to let Mrs Markham home at her usual time and about never leaving the children alone.

Sometimes the evenings were long. When the light lingered and she grew tired of her few tapes and bored (as she'd always been) by television, she sometimes went in to check that the children were all right and at such times their sleeping faces seemed to her defenceless and even beautiful. Andrew's anyway. Once, with the bathroom windows wide open, she stripped off all her clothes and examined her body in the filtered green light from the park. It was still, as it had always been, lean, long-waisted and small-breasted with ribs showing and the hip bones a bit spiky. He hadn't liked them. Said he preferred the Juno type but for some reason Junos were a bit thin (ha ha) on the ground this year. It was the thirties-style clothes that had everyone slimmed down to the bone. His last lady before leaving home had been a pretty cow, however, lush where biologically necessary. Una said he wasn't exactly her type either. She preferred a little more brains, less brawn, and a lot more energy. The jokes were known by both to be rather more than half serious. There was no question of a love affair. Simply both had other plans which came to nothing and they had somehow been thrown together that term in college. Sometimes they made one another laugh and there had never been any question of telling him she was pregnant. That would have been the biggest joke of all.

What worried her about having the abortion was a trivial thing really. After a long enjoyable shower, she examined her body again in the green light. What worried her was giving it voluntarily over for storming. She knew that afterwards it felt like no more than a heavy period. That's all it was really. Nothing. Accidental fertilisation of an egg, unplanned multiplication of little cells, a bit more than the womb lining to shed at the end of six weeks or so. That was all. Sometimes it happened naturally and then people got upset if they happened to be married and happened to want a child. The actual abortion thing itself was expensive and a nuisance and she didn't like the thought of surrendering herself for money to other people, blindly taking their skills for granted because that was all one could do. She thought it more than likely she'd feel exactly the same about a birth. That was a sort of surrender too and you were prepared by clinical hands as for an operation, the way her sister had been.

She got angry all over again when she remembered the stupid way it happened: carelessness about going in time for another prescription. A few days without pills and he had to take her to a party, to a place she'd never been before, near Celbridge where he lived. He knew his way well around the house and eventually had led her to a little room above the stables with a small square window showing moonlight on the cobblestones. He hadn't put on the light and he had difficulty opening the window. The room smelled musty at first but it was late May and the window soon let in the scents of lilac and hawthorn and she hadn't seen him for a while. Nor, as a matter of fact, did she want to see him ever again. Even during the bumpy drive back to town in the back seat of a little Fiat designed for midgets, she knew she was pregnant. Maybe you always knew. Her mother had said *she* always knew and she'd been pregnant eight times. It was, her mother said, God's will. But God's will permitted contraceptives to be invented also and now it seemed rational to make the bearing of a child (whether in marriage or outside it) one's own will also. Once more she examined her body, imagining the gross changes of late pregnancy, the darkened milky nipples, the misshapen belly; worst of all the sinister pencil-blue stretchmarks which (if one lived to be a hundred, her mother said) would never go away. Compulsively she took another shower, revelling in the warm mist of water in whose orbit she was happy again, as she supposed the embryo was happy in its watery element. Dry and dressed again, she went once more to count the pay cheques with which freedom would be bought.

Still Life

SYLVIA was nineteen, and it was a country Sam, her host, knew nothing about. Gradually he learned a little.

He learned that there were some letters that ought not to be presented before breakfast and one that couldn't be left until afterwards. He learned when an invitation to join him and his wife Rosemary would be welcome and when Sylvia had to be left alone. He learned to read her strange pale face as a countryman reads the sky. Storms seldom took him by surprise towards the end of her second year in college, and for hours Rosemary and he discussed nothing but what was related in one way or another to their charge. Rosemary was in some ways a better interpreter although her interest tended to flag at times and incomprehensibly she would switch off. The conversation one spring night began as casually as all the others.

"Do you think I should give Sylvia the message or not?" Sam said.

"Possibly."

"Or would it merely upset her having to make a decision?"

"Possibly."

"What am I talking about?" Sam asked.

"I haven't the faintest idea. But since you ask me it must have something to do with Sylvia, mustn't it?"

He had to put up with an increasing amount of irony these days but it didn't bother him. He presumed that his wife liked to keep her wit sharpened for the benefit of her pupils in junior school.

"Could you just give this your attention for one moment?"

"Very well." A sigh. A toss of the head.

"I was wondering whether I should convey the message

of this fellow Tony or not. That he'll be in O'Dwyer's until ten o'clock. Michael is supposed to be calling at nine."

"Well, did you tell Tony that you'd give the message?"

"Not in so many words. I asked him if there *was* any message." What was it about this simple statement of fact that made Rosemary fall around laughing?

"My God, slippery as the traditional Jesuit, aren't you – how has it escaped my notice all these years?"

"Can't you be serious for one moment? It would be much better for Sylvia if she did *not* go to O'Dwyer's."

"But you are hardly the person who should decide, are you?"

"It's a question of responsibility. I don't like the look of that fellow. You said yourself that he carries around a seducer's rug knitted for him out of two tons of wool by his grandmother. What sort of fellow seems to know by radar or something when a girl is harmlessly deciding to spend a sunny afternoon with her books in the garden on a day we both happen to be out and even my parents are both down the country at a wedding? What sort of fellow would scream up the road in that sports car and step out of it without opening the door but with that rug slung across one arm?"

"It could be that such a fellow had been informed by his lady that the coast was going to be clear," said Rosemary blandly.

"It couldn't. You know Sylvia is no slyboots."

"Sylvia is nearly twenty and quite capable of codding us as naturally as she would her parents. We are, as the lawyers say, *in loco parentis*."

"You know that isn't true. We're her friends."

"But we represent authority, as her mother knew we would when she sent her to stay with us. It's all right so long as *we* don't abuse it. So I think you should deliver that message."

"Mother thinks I shouldn't."

"Oh, you and your mother! You should beware of taking *her* advice about Sylvia. The girl will simply move out.

Finale. Speaking for myself, I don't care one way or the other, but you mightn't like it." She turned her face away so he couldn't see her expression, but her words startled him. The prospect of Sylvia's moving out had never occurred to him.

"The point is, Rosemary, she might learn to like Michael as much as he likes her if she gave him half a chance. And it would surely be better for her."

"You say that because you think he's harmless. He may play the recorder like an angel and look like a Teddy Bear and he may call you Sir ten times every five minutes, but none of that would stop him being as much of an opportunist as Tony once the door was shut behind him. Look, either you're going to buy a lock and chain or a chastity belt and be her jailer if that's what you want or you're going to leave the girl alone to build her own defences if that's what she wants. Listen, there's a party down in Baggot Street tonight. We're both invited. I left it to the last moment to ask you so you couldn't think up any excuse."

"I think I'd prefer to hold on here. Mother and Father are for once going to the movies."

"So you'll wait on here for cries of help, will you?"

"Please don't be silly. I simply feel there should be somebody in the house."

"You simply don't want to come to the party this time either – isn't that it?"

"All right. I don't want to come to the party. Thanks all the same."

"For nothing, Sam."

"I'm sorry, Rosemary."

"My mother died when I was seven," she said with sudden fierceness. This was not news to Sam, but the next line was, which after fifteen years of marriage he supposed was surprising enough.

They had reached the stage when each could foresee the stories of the other as one can foresee the moves in a chess game. *He* knew her student holiday around Italy as though it had been his own, and he knew exactly at what point in any sociable evening she would come up with her worst hitch-hiking experience, with the theft of her laboriously-made Michelangelo sketches, with the day her youngest brother decided to join the travellers against the advice of Jem Connors himself. He winced in company before each story as he supposed she must wince before each of his. But this particular night, all dressed up for a party and giving off sparks, she surprised him, after fifteen years.

"I tell myself and sometimes other people that I remember all sorts of things about my mother, but do you know all I actually do remember? That she had black hair like mine and that one day after I had *forced* myself to apologise to her for tearing a dress the second day in succession while I was climbing trees with my brother, she said to me: 'If you were sorry, Rosemary, you wouldn't do it.' She must have said thousands of other things to me in seven years but that's all I remember and I thought it the stupidest remark I ever heard. But now I think it would be relevant if I said it to you. I won't say it, however. I'll say, goodnight, Sam."

When she had gone, skipping down the steps to the car faster than usual as though she feared he might follow her, she left a sort of hollowness behind, a pain that was difficult to define but persisted until heavy clogs tramped up the steps and Sylvia let herself in.

"Any messages, Sam?"

"Any expected?"

"Not really. I'm totally exhausted after five solid hours in the library and I'm having an early night."

"You haven't forgotten about Michael?"

"Oh God, not tonight. It isn't tonight, Sam?"

"I'm afraid so."

"Be a lamb and talk to him for half an hour and send him home happy."

"He's coming to see *you*."

"Never mind that. I have to wash my hair before going to bed. I've had five hours of bugs – think of it, Samuel, and have pity."

"I have pity."

"Saintly Sam. You know there are only seven of us taking bacteriology, but did you know we go by a low generic term invented by the others?"

"It was the same in my day. It's always been the same, Sylvia."

"The buggers. True in a couple of cases, perhaps, but not all. Saintly Sam, good night."

"You really do look tired out, Sylvia. Leave the hair until tomorrow and go straight to bed."

"I can't leave the hair until tomorrow because tomorrow Tony may telephone and the hair has to be ready, don't you see?"

All right, Rosemary down in Baggot Street, all right. You win. I can't do it.

"My God, I really am losing my memory by rapid stages. Tony did ring. Said he'd be in O'Dwyers until ten. You can phone him at once and say you'll see him tomorrow."

"What you're really losing is your *mind*, Samuel. I'm off. Do I look like a clapped-out cow? Who cares? Had I better go up quickly and change, though?"

"I suppose you'd better." What was the use of arguing? With closed eyes he listened to a bath being run, heard her scampering from one heap of clothes in her chaotic room to another. In exactly fifteen minutes she was down to say goodbye, black-rimmed eyes glimmering from the newly-made silvery face, smiling.

"Sam, my friend, goodnight. Give nice Michael my regards and send him home happy. And for God's sake wish me luck."

"Good luck, Sylvia." With what, Sylvia? For the second time that night he heard the hall door slamming shut and then he waited for the footsteps of nice Michael.

An unusual thing happened after Michael had gone away happy, so far as one could judge. Sam was climbing up to his room around midnight when his father called to him on the first landing. Somewhat puzzled, he stepped into the room which was full of shadows except for the area surrounding the brass table lamp whose shade was white and translucent as an eggshell, like the old face in fact. The old man was on for talk, for a long session of dull rememberings. Sam listened for a while, irritated and moved at the same time, noting the recurrent name of Rosemary, whom the old man described as "all the daughters your mother and I hoped for and never had until now, and a good wife too, Sam." When the time came for him to snuff out, the old man said, and the next heart attack would do it, he'd like to go knowing that Sam would always appreciate her for the unusual person she was and not waste his time running after a fast young one who was nothing to any of them and no better than she ought to be if the truth were known. This was the once-removed-peasant-made-good, whom Sam had half-despised all his life, yet never escaped from, whose business he would inherit as a sort of eternal connection which he thought would feel stronger than paternity. He knew there was something else he ought to say before saying goodnight, but how could the words be found? Mind your own bloody business, old father, for as long as you can mind it, and I'll mind mine. But also, pardon, old father. In fact, bless me father for I have sinned before heaven and before thee, sins of omission, hundreds of them. Now I'm sorry because you are going to die and when you are dead I'll have to be a person in my own right because there is nobody else to be a person even in time to come. No son to prove your blood and mine and pardon, old father, because I truly never wanted one. She said if I did she could have had one like everybody else and she's probably right.

He hardly listened when his father urged him to look into the room upstairs before going to bed, but he answered mechanically all the same. "Very well, father, I will. Goodnight now."

Rosemary's studio had been built as a sort of lean-to extension to this top storey so that you opened a door at the top of the stairs and stepped abruptly into a room the size of a barn. Its open glass walls let in the night, a blurry moon, a scatter of dim stars, a murmur from nearby poplar trees like the faraway sound of the sea. For some reason he flinched from switching on the light – anyway where was the need?

He could see the heaped-up canvases in every corner and a half-finished oil set up on its easel facing the main north light. He could see quite clearly the usual clutter of a painter's workroom, brushes standing on flat surfaces everywhere, old cloths rolled in balls and clotted with paint and up on the specially constructed shelves the strange objects Rosemary liked to surround herself with: a long-dried hydrangea head which would certainly crumble to dust at a touch, several chunks of granite and oddly shaped flints, the unexplained handlebars of a child's scooter, one of those glass balls fishermen used to float their nets, a black doll's head, a wine-glass full of – of what?

He touched a switch and light flooded down from two huge lamps his father had bought her which could simulate daylight very well. What *was* in the glass? A purplish mess, hairy with mould in places, with some sort of liquid in the bottom. He carried it over to the nearest lamp – although with this sort of light it wasn't necessary – but it was only when he touched the stuff that he realised what it was. Old grapeskins with the warm bloom of distant mountains on them where the mould had not yet settled. Why had she kept them? Was it a mad effort to make a glass of wine? Was this what his father meant?

A night bird blundered against the lighted glass and the loud rap of its beak had something alarming in the violence of it. He stared down into the wine glass, uneasy, and then over at the canvas stretched on its frame. Of course. Of course. She had kept the grapeskins for their colour. There it was reproduced in oil paint left of centre; presumably this canvas was going to be an abstract landscape. Perhaps not even a bad one, although he had tried to tell her often enough that her special talent was for teaching and that it was better to be a good teacher than an indifferent painter.

In the white candid light he examined what she had done. Not much, and really not much better than usual. Leaning close to examine the texture, his fingers came to rest on the table beside the easel on which were piled palette and paints she had used and was going to use. Straightening up again, he noticed his fingertips covered in thick dust, the light furry dust of a place usually kept clean. When the message reached his reluctant brain he stood quite still, then moved from one surface to another running his fingers along it and watching the drifts of dust rise and then settle again in the strong light.

She couldn't have been here for weeks – months, more likely. Pain strummed in his temples again with sudden violence and he switched off the light, which now seemed indecent in its clarity. Downstairs, as he closed the door of Rosemary's studio, the hall clock struck two and the house turned over in its sleep. It would be a long time before Sylvia or Rosemary came home.

End of the Line

It's the raspberries I remember best about that summer. There never was such a crop and I knew that Mr Bentley had decided to build his entire entertaining around them for a while. He phoned me one day and (obliquely as ever) giggling slightly, intimated that he still had far too many raspberries and we would have to help him out with them again. Who else was coming? I could hear the caution in my own voice, even although I knew that Mr Bentley's parties of one sort or another were rarely intolerable. It was just that he had made himself responsible for quite a few dull people who were so obsessed with their own problems that they tended to drive other people away. Would I care to bring Jerry along as a peace gesture, Mr Bentley asked suddenly, and he giggled uneasily when I said I certainly would not. He said no more except that if Saturday would suit me it would be fine for him and not to bother eating before I arrived some time around midday.

Mr Bentley lived where he had always lived ever since I was at school and went to him for extra piano lessons. He lived in a large stone house of amazing ugliness except for the largely wild garden. You approached it through a leafy gap between numbers eighteen and twenty of a handsome road in Donnybrook. Almost immediately you found yourself confronting the remains of a beautiful ironwork gate with 'Hazeldene' enscrolled on it. This could be confusing to a newcomer because it was not the entrance to a conventional driveway. Elegantly designed bungalows were scattered to right and left behind their screens of copper beech or poplar. Some of them dated from the nineteen-twenties and most of them were supposed to be guarded by the large somnolent dogs who lifted a lazy eye at strange footsteps and sometimes came over wagging their tails. Everywhere there was the silence of all those trees and you felt vaguely that if there had to be bungalows there they should have been Indian Empire style with maybe a dozing ayah rocking in the porch and the breathing jungle just a short distance away in the intense heat.

There was nothing colonial in that sense about Mr Bentley's home when you came upon it at last in its circular gravelled drive. It was large, Cromwellian-looking and fortressy, made of cut-stone that had seen better days – lichens had invaded it and the dampness had made strange colours and patterns on the wall. A dead Virginia creeper still held on with its bleached white arms. Partly wild since the last live-in family gardener had been put away into a home and the last ffrench-Morris had died in Bournemouth it was, thanks to Mr Bentley, a paradise garden in other parts. There were rose beds that I could smell as soon as I stepped onto the drive and there were little brilliant shrubberies scooped out of the brambles and bamboos, which blazed with jonquils and crocuses in early spring. In summer there were big flowering things like hydrangeas which took care of themselves and there was every imaginable kind of heather. Each time Mr Bentley made another border or shrubbery he had to ask formal permission through the solicitors of the present owner, a building contractor who maintained distant but good terms with the few remaining tenants. Nobody had ever had to fend off a bribe to quit, but it was noticeable that there were no new lettings either. Mr Bentley had been given (on a mere request) permission to use some of the empty rooms for entertaining in whenever he wished, and I can remember a few good Christmas parties in gaunt candlelit rooms which he had transformed as though they were stage sets with trailing ivy and red ribbons.

His own flat was small and dusty and largely taken over by his grand piano and his bookshelves. He had never lived anywhere else since his mother died and left their joint home to a more favoured son in Canada. It was to this small flat I used to come as a schoolgirl, drawn in the right direction that first time by the hesitant tinkle of scales coming through the trees. Mr Bentley was firm as well as patient. Many of his students eventually won prizes and some of them were concert performers now.

I found him beaming among the raspberry canes from which a gentle steam was rising after last night's rain.

"They love it," he assured me. "Heat and moisture combined. They keep coming and ripening for me – pick a bowlful for breakfast and you have more berries on those same bushes for dinner. Welcome, Anna." His tufted white hair stood up straight on his head and his eyes were kind and blue as cornflowers. His wrecked teeth ought to have looked ugly but instead his smile was something people remembered. There was nothing in his face to suggest the disciplinarian that lurked behind it. "Find a bowl over there and come and help me, Anna."

I did as I was told although I would have preferred to sit on a fallen tree trunk and lift my face to the sun. I had always liked to close my eyes and listen to his garden. Bees among the roses and the fading cotoneaster blossoms. A grasshopper somewhere. The river rattling on over its pebbles at the end of the wall. The stretching and sighing of trees especially in the heat. But I knew this garden in every season. I liked it best in the depths of summer although I can hardly remember an idle moment there. I remember weeding, watering, dead-heading, picking roses for the house. I remember cutting shrubs back after flowering to strengthen them for next summer. All that.

"Who's coming?"

He gave me a name and I sighed.

"A very talented woman," he said firmly. "A very difficult life which she has triumphantly organised."

"That's her trouble," I sighed again. "Organisation. Who else?" He told me. It was going to be one of those days.

"I can't stay very long," I said.

"But all the same I know you will, Anna. I need your help. Besides it's a special day."

"Every day is a special day to you," I grumbled and then gave myself up to the enjoyment of the raspberries themselves, so fragile in their ripeness, so moist and soft that they needed feather fingers to pick them. Piano fingers. I looked from my several ruined berries into Mr Bentley's bowl of beauties and then I looked down at his bony hands, no flesh anywhere except at the soft fingertips lightly coloured by the juices which he had not spilled. Mr Bentley would never be coarse the way my own father loved to be at times. "Handle those pears as tenderly as though they were virgins," he said to me once, to be instantly reproved by my mother. I went on picking berries in silent companionship for a long time, fingers tingling with the fine little thorny needles which protected the fruit. "You made me forget what I was about to do when you arrived," Mr Bentley said, and before going into the house he took and emptied my half-full bowl into his own and gave it back to me. I went on picking, conscious now of the winey smell of the fruit as the sun strengthened to a burning point on the back of my neck. I had always felt secure in this garden, indeed in Mr Bentley's company. It was a place where I liked to come to forget the person I really was. When he came back he put an old straw hat on my head and another even more battered on his own. He had carried them one inside the other under one arm and an old portable gramophone (the sort you wind up) hung from the other. He had forgotten to bring back his bowl, so I went around to fetch that and even from indoors, in the chill gloom, I could hear the ravishing music, vaguely familiar and improved if anything by the tinny soundbox of the old machine. I looked around at the tidy details of Mr Bentley's kitchen, his clean tea towels hanging up on the hooks, his big bowls of prepared salads, his plait of garlic hung from the casement window frame and his rows of spices. The music got louder and tinnier as I neared the raspberry canes and I found him standing with eyes closed and a sweet smile on his face.

"Tod und Verklaren, Anna," he said, shaking his head, and resuming his picking. "One of the divinest sounds of this century. Strauss wrote it when he was a strippling, you'll remember – what could he have known then of death and transfiguration? In fact he knew everything and the proof is (or I believe it is) that he reworked some of those themes into the *Last Songs* completed the year of his death. Sit down for a minute and listen. We have plenty of time to finish our picking before the others arrive."

So we sat down on a once-white garden seat and listened to the aching sweetness of the music that follows the troubled opening bars.

"Don't cry, Anna, but tell me about it," Mr Bentley said. "Why don't you go back to your husband and see how it will be? You married him, after all. Things go wrong but the basic feeling must remain, I think. I don't, of course, know," he said modestly, patting my hand kindly.

"No you don't, Mr Bentley. We were married two years ago and already all that is over. He slurped his soup and grunted like a pig in bed and never came to the Concert Hall any more. And he only took one shower a week – every Saturday night – and he left his cigarette butts in the handbasin and he never disguised the fact that he hated my cat. Once he went home with a MAN after we'd gone out together to a party and he got somebody else to give me a lift home."

Silenced by this time, Mr Bentley looked dismayed at me for a moment before replying delicately.

"I hope he's careful about his health. That sort of life is very dangerous these times as we all know but you may be mistaken. Maybe if you had a baby," Mr Bentley said wistfully. "After a check-up for both of you, of course."

"No THANK you," I shuddered with genuine horror. "You're a dear but you're so wrong it's pathetic. Let's get back to the raspberries."

"I'll talk to you later, Anna," Mr Bentley said gently. "Dry your eyes." He gave me one of his usual spotless handkerchiefs (did he do his own laundry too?) and we went back to our picking.

Delius appeared suddenly from the vegetable patch

where he may have been lying asleep and licked my bare legs affectionately. He's an old once-white Scotch terrier who doesn't smell too good any more but he's part of Hazeldene and I've known him a long time. He ate a raspberry Mr Bentley offered him and he must be the only dog in the world who would do that. As we worked he waddled to the garden seat and lay down there in the shade of it, nose between his paws.

"It isn't as though I had any talent to fall back on," I said, coming to the middle row Mr Bentley and I were picking together, and suddenly looking into his face I knew if I'd had the choice of a father this is the man I would select to be mine. If he weren't basically so truthful he would have reassured me now but I wouldn't be interested in that sort of reassurance.

"You will always play to the great pleasure of those listening to you in a domestic setting," Mr Bentley said kindly. "That's not nothing, Anna. And if you can refrain from being so hard on yourself you will always play for your own considerable pleasure too. Will you not be satisfied as I had to be so long ago when I opted for teaching and *that* turned out to be a source of lifelong joy to me?"

He smiled his beautiful smile again under the old straw hat and it didn't matter that the teeth were gapped in his upper jaw while in his lower jaw they were worn down like those of an old horse. I shook my head and looked away and the old gramophone rattled into silence.

"Look, here's another treat for you," he said. "Listen to this. I think you haven't heard the Lucia Popp recording of the *Last Songs*."

The voice is beautiful beyond measure and so are the songs but I don't think anybody can ever have heard them to such advantage as I did that July afternoon in Mr Bentley's garden. They are voluptuous, languishing songs and the way she sings them makes you know it's all over.

But I wasn't going to cry again in view of the voices from the front of the house announcing the arrival of all those dull people whose problems would be placed before Mr Bentley whenever the chance arose. Sometimes you could see them watching for it. But I'll say this for them. They fell upon the meat ready for carving and they set about all the remaining work and they even carried out the kitchen table to place under the chestnut tree where everything was laid out temptingly in the shade. One of the women had brought a freshly baked salmon which she had done herself and another had whipped bowls of the cream they had brought for the raspberries. A particularly tiresome man had brought a bottle of gin – it was more usual to bring wine – because he said it improved the flavour of the raspberries. While we ate the wafers of beautifully carved beef (there was a master carver among the friends too) and the salmon and all the salads Mr Bentley had prepared, the raspberries lay bathing in a whole cupful of gin in a large blue bowl, their colour dimmed by a light dusting of castor sugar. I prefer raspberries with no sweetness but their own, but naturally the woman who had triumphantly organised her very difficult life had sugared them. Nevertheless, eaten with ice-cold Muscadet, they were very good. Nobody who hasn't been given raspberries straight from the canes within an hour of picking knows what raspberries should taste like. Strawberries by comparison are mundane. It's true they come first but by the time summer is at its height, they are already turnipy and flavourless. Raspberries are the true fruits of midsummer, and it was in Mr Bentley's garden that I first tasted them as they should be eaten. The taste of ripe raspberries at the moment when they melt between your teeth is what I remember best of that summer and I have reason to remember that summer.

After lunch we lay around on the grass which earlier in the day had been cool and damp and was now parched by the sun. My shorts and tee shirt looked absurd among the elaborate summer dresses of the women but that was how I had planned to look, among them but not of them. They all recoiled from Delius when he ambled around offering his welcome, and eventually the dog settled himself against my legs, his old fur smelly, scratchy and hot. But I could do that much for him if he liked to be there. He rewarded me by caressing my wrist with a cold black nose, surprisingly moist and healthy. I could have lain in that garden forever, giving nothing except to the dog, listening to the bees in the lime trees to my left, to the rattling unseen river, to Mr Bentley's reasonable soft voice offering advice, even a solution or two. I wished they would all go away, especially the gin man who wanted to know where my husband was. Eventually they did go, but not before the sun was low and thick and golden along the grass, not before they had carried everything back into the house including the table and put the kitchen to rights again. That's the kind of people they are. The gin man was the last to go after he had played Chopin softly and abominably on Mr Bentley's grand piano and invited me to accompany him to the theatre that night because he had a spare ticket. When I refused he went away civilly enough.

This had always been my time of day in the garden. We didn't talk very much. We rambled around picking up morsels of food or the odd paper napkin off the grass although truly the guests had tidied up pretty well.

We wandered over to a rose bed at exactly the hour when roses are at their best, breathing out the accumulated heat of the day, practically ready to talk to you. Almost all of Mr Bentley's roses were old-fashioned, chosen for their exact shape and colour but also for their perfumes. They shaded from creamy white at the edges of the circular bed through to pink and crimson and yellow and, at the centre, a few almost black roses. I liked the floppy pink tea roses best. Mr Bentley preferred what he called Crimson Glory, deeply red and velvety and smelling of heaven but with a tendency to hang its head in full bloom. You had to lift it up to look at it. "Let's take a bunch of these up to Mrs Aylmer," Mr Bentley said suddenly, "and the rest of the raspberries. But wait, before we do we must water the roses and then I want to show you something, Anna."

Watering roses after a long hot day is never a chore. They seem to stretch up and offer themselves for spraying, and even the droopers sometimes lift their heads. Saying he would cut Mrs Aylmer's roses when they dried off a bit, Mr Bentley led the way past his vegetable garden and through a wilderness of brambles and thistles to a little clearing near the river wall. Here he indicated a few straggling green plants which seemed to me quite unremarkable. But Mr Bentley smiled triumphantly.

"Planted them last autumn and always forgot to show you. Hazels, Anna. In years to come in this soft wet soil there will be hazelnuts for the picking and nobody will ever know or enjoy them except for a few gallant explorers from your old school! Imagine a Hazeldene without hazels!" he chuckled. "And yet I believe this garden has been without hazel bushes since it was laid out some hundred and fifty years ago, the time the house was built. Of course it could have been called after a lady named Hazel'."

"That was a brilliant idea to plant those," I said, smiling at him. He looked down quite shyly in acknowledgement and giggled. Then he went back to cut the roses and on into the house to feed Delius.

The house which could be icy cold in winter seemed to hold all the heat of the long summer's day as we climbed up the neglected staircase to Mrs Aylmer's. On both landings we passed tall windows overlooking the river and the setting sun. Its light filtered strangely through the dusty panels of deep blue and gold glass, and it changed Mr Bentley's face quite suddenly into that of an old man. I shivered slightly. There would be a long warm twilight when the sun went down, he predicted. Maybe if I wasn't in any hurry I might like to play a Bach trio with him before we made supper? We could forget about the viola and he'd play the fiddle to my piano. We would leave the window wide open and Mrs Aylmer could listen too. Her room was just above his, these two floors up.

There was an amazing blood-red sunset flooding across

Mrs Aylmer's landing but no answer when we knocked at her door. The brass plate was handsome and brightly polished and it said FLORENCE AYLMER SPEECH THERAPIST CONSULTATIONS BY APPOINTMENT. Was it because we hadn't an appointment that there was no answer, I wondered flippantly, but Mr Bentley was very worried, quite pale, I noticed, in a moment. He called "Florence!" several times and then asked me to wait while he went down to fetch the spare key she had given him "in case of emergencies". This, it seemed, was an emergency. I walked over to the window and felt the warmth of the last light of the day washing over me. I was irritated with Florence Aylmer whom I had never met because she was intruding by her silence. I noticed Mr Bentley had taken away his red roses and his raspberries as though he didn't expect to be able to deliver them. He was not.

We found Mrs Aylmer who was large and very old fallen sideways in her bed, her face purplish and her hands cold, but she was not dead. The oriental beauty and order of her room seemed in strange contrast to the ungainly figure. Mr Bentley tried his best to rouse her but he failed and he asked me to phone 999 for an ambulance while he stayed with her. I tried to feel pity for this unknown old woman, speech therapist and widow of an art collector, young once and maybe beautiful, maybe even happy, but all I could feel was irritation that a lovely day which had not ended was now apparently over.

The ambulance men with great speed and efficiency arrived and carried her downstairs on a stretcher, all wrapped up in blankets, and I watched in the driveway as they settled Mrs Aylmer into the ambulance, slammed the doors, got Mr Bentley to sign a paper and drove away under the trees. When I looked again at Mr Bentley I saw that he was shaking although his face seemed as immobile as the old lady's. I wondered if perhaps they had been lovers long ago or even before Mrs Aylmer had become so crippled with arthritis, but the more I thought about it the less likely it seemed.

"I'll make you a cup of tea," I said, smiling at him because it seemed the only thing I could do for him but he said, "No, Anna, no. We'll have a drop of something stronger tonight."

In the dusky music room he lifted down a bottle of whiskey from his wall cabinet and then he took down two heavy crystal glasses. I'd never seen him drink anything but wine before and I myself connected whiskey with two things only, hot lemony punch for winter colds as a child and the swinish snoring of my husband after futile attempts at copulation several nights a week. But I suddenly discovered I too was cold, because that was how Mr Bentley was. He handed me my glass with a hand that was still shaking and we sipped the hot spirit together without speaking. After several swallows Mr Bentley's drink was almost gone and he poured a little more into the glasses before replacing his bottle in the cupboard.

"Poor Florence," he said. "Poor Florence. If only I'd come up earlier, as I'd intended to –"

"No," I said. "It wouldn't have made any difference. You know it wouldn't."

"Perhaps you're right." He sighed as he switched on a lamp that had a dusty deep yellow shade but also he smiled at me.

"You know, Anna, I think this is the actual end of the line for this old house."

"How do you mean?" My heart dropped like a stone, and I felt like a dreamer who has missed several steps on the stairway. He smiled again, sipped his whiskey as though nothing were the matter and then he took a letter out of his pocket.

"I told you this was a special day, Anna. It's special because this came by post this morning."

Before I read it I knew exactly what it would say. Donlon and Company, Building Contractors, had instructed the writer to thank Mr Bentley for his careful attention in every respect to their property, but they now felt it was time to offer both him and Mrs Aylmer alternative accommodation in one of their developed properties.

"A service flat!" I said, shocked even before I finished reading the letter. He would find that the owners would be more than generous in the matter of rent in view of his long tenancy of a ground-floor apartment at Hazeldene but of course if he preferred to make his own arrangements about alternative accommodation there would be a sum of money forthcoming to compensate for the disturbance. The solicitor strongly advised Mr Bentley to go along with the first suggestion which in his opinion would be financially advantageous. He would be pleased to discuss personally etc.

Something suddenly struck me as I folded up the letter.

"Did Mrs Aylmer get one of those this morning?"

"Yes she did. She phoned me and I went up to her. She was shattered. She's been a tenant here for thirty years, ever since her husband died."

"Don't you think this may have had something to do with –"

"I'm sure of it."

"She's old," I said, anxious to convince myself as well as him. "It might have happened anyway. You're *much* younger, and I know it's awful but you'll, you'll . . ."

There it was, I was crying again, and Mr Bentley, far more normal-looking now after the drink, was looking as concerned as ever for me.

"I'll be perfectly all right wherever I go – of course I will. Once I have transported my piano and my books and all my junk, what does the place matter? Home can be remade anywhere, Anna."

I know it was disgraceful, utterly shameful, but I was crying for myself now.

"Your new hazel bushes!" I howled. "Your raspberries and your roses and your vegetable patch. It's not FAIR!"

"Do you know, Anna, if they have a tither of wit they'll leave the roses and the trees and some at least of the little wilderness beside the river and then they can sell more expensive houses. Bet you they'll call them town houses of character and quality in a secluded woodland setting within ten minutes of the city centre. What do you bet?" said Mr Bentley, looking almost mischievous now. "Come on, Anna, dry your eyes and what's more important dry your *fingers*, my dear, and sit down at the piano. Why shouldn't we have our little night music after all, and then we can make supper and take Delius for his walk at the same time as we leave you most of the way home."

"Home?" I said, again shamefully, "I have no home but this."

Mr Bentley didn't appear to hear me. He was tuning his fiddle, seemingly quite absorbed and happy. Forcing my memory now I still have no clear recollection of the music, whether I played badly or well. What I remember of that last day at Hazeldene are the warm raspberries and their exact texture as they burst between your teeth, Tod und Verklaren on the old scratchy gramophone and the sun burning the back of my neck until Mr Bentley's old hat gave me its healing shade.